Fear
Unleashed

Book 1

Lynnie DN

UPDRAFT LITERARY

Published by Updraft Literary
Cover design and interior illustrations by Marina Price
ISBN: 979-8-9992421-0-5
Printed in the United States of America

First Edition

For Esmé

You changed my world in ways you'll only understand when you're grown.

May you face the world with open arms and a fearless heart.

CONTENTS

1. The Foamula 1

2. Something Wicked, Something Weak 8

3. Echoes in the Stone 12

4. The Girl Who Read the Words 15

5. The Escape 19

6. The Entire Department 27

7. The Door and the Deal 30

8. The Ghost Room 34

9. Above it All 40

10. The Weak Link 49

11. Jump! 53

12. Hay There 56

13. Rise of the Mukdri 60

14. Mostly Hay 64

15. The Path Not Chosen 69

16. Stalked 73

17. Nothing to See Here 80

18. Nightfall   83

19. Unlikely Allies   91

20. Into the Woods   96

21. Crickets and Blood   101

22. The River to Acoena   104

23. Just Breathe   118

24. What Remains   125

25. Everything is Alive   129

26. Waking Dreams   132

27. The Leash   137

28. Becoming a Magi   141

29. Gathering the Broken   146

30. First Star   152

31. Flint! Flint! Flint!   157

32. The Dark Path   160

33. Not Yet   164

34. Left Was the Plan   168

35. Where Dreams Lead   173

36. The Pack   180

37. Into the Darkness   183

38. No Way Back   191

Pronunciation Guide   199

Map of Maead   201

Acknowledgements   202

Community / Author   204

1

THE FOAMULA

With the twitch of her finger, Opal would be six again. She tapped the screen of the vidframe, and the picture began to move. She watched herself curled on her mother's lap in her pajamas.

"And then we'll all live way up high in a space house. I just have to find the right formula."

"You need foam to go to space?" Opal's extended finger moved dangerously close to her nose.

The picture jiggled as her dad silently laughed behind the camera.

"What? No." Her mom gently caught the impending nose pick and pulled her hand away. "Not foam. Formula. The fuel we're using blows up too easily. We need a new mixture."

"Oh. And then we can go live in space?"

"Not right away. First, we have to build a place to live. Then you, me, and Daddy can move to the stars and watch Maead spin underneath us while I study space."

"But won't we fall back down?"

"No." Her mom kissed the top of her head, "The houses we build will have little rockets on them, to keep us in orbit."

"Once you fix the foamula."

"The formula, yes."

"Maybe I can help someday. Maybe I'll know how to do the formula." Her tongue worked hard to make the 'r' sound, and she almost succeeded.

"You just might, my little scientist. Now, off to bed."

"I can't wait to go to sleep in space."

She jumped off her mom's lap, bouncing down the hallway. The image froze mid-leap, capturing her mid-air, weightless.

And just like that, Opal was thirteen again. She wiped away the tears pooling on her lower lids. That was the last video her dad had taken of them together, one that might've been deleted if her mom hadn't died a few days later while working on the explosive fuel.

Without warning, the video reset to the image of Opal on her mom's lap. She brushed a fingertip across her mom's face on the screen and whispered, "I'm sorry, Mom. I tried. I don't know what else to do."

She laid the vidframe face down on the dresser, as if shielding her mom from seeing what her life had become. Then she scanned her bedroom.

A poster of rollerboarder Miles Miller doing a Zylo flip off the grav-mod ramp was pinned to the wall. She could look at him all day. Her plastic rollerboard sat in the corner, gathering dust. She missed going to the roller park but didn't want to be seen with that kiddie board. The cardboard spacescope she and her dad had built, back when they still got along was propped up nearby. She wished she could stay here forever, surrounded by her favorite things.

Instead, she sighed and left her bedroom.

Her dad was whistling at the stove. Still in his pajamas, he was making pancakes.

"So, are you nervous?" he asked, sliding a couple of pancakes onto her plate.

"What do you think?"

"Yes, but now you'll be around other kids like you."

"Weird kids," she muttered.

"Arcane kids. Special kids."

"Yeah, in a useless, sucky way that everybody makes fun of."

"Not in your new school. Just wait. It'll be incredible."

"The only way it will be incredible is if my new school is Deullen Middle Grades," Opal said.

"I'm sorry," her dad said. "I know you had your heart set on going into space."

"I actually had the test scores to do it. It's going to happen in the next ten years, and it could have been me. It's not fair."

Her father flipped another pancake and dropped it onto her plate.

"I know you can't see it now, but it is fair. You tested even higher in magic than in science, and Pascam Middle Grades is what the council decided was best for everyone. Andrin needs people like you."

Opal really didn't care if they needed her. She was a scientist, not a mage.

Even though she could barely look at him, she humored him when he walked her outside to take the first-day-of-school picture.

"I really hope your attitude improves. You might not understand now, but this is what's best. We haven't had a really good mage in a long time. We have plenty of scientists."

"Yeah, let me spend years studying so I can make a flame on the end of my finger when I could just flip the light switch, read my physics books, and improve the world."

Her dad studied the picture he'd just taken on his old handcom. He was so arcane; he didn't even have a wristcom.

"Can we take another one?" he asked. "You look so angry." He flipped the screen around to show her.

Her straight, blond hair wasn't styled. She wore a T-shirt from a popular show years ago, and her denims were also outdated. And her face? Her dad was right. There was anger in her eyes.

"Good. I am angry. Because Mom wouldn't have let the placement board send me to Pascam. She would have made sure I studied something that matters, like science or math. I wouldn't have to go to my first day of school looking like this. Mom wouldn't have let any of this happen."

Part of her wanted to hurt him, but a bigger part of her didn't want to see his face when it landed. She spun around and stomped away.

After walking several blocks, she descended into the bright, white, electric world of the New Andrin subway. The train to the old industrial district was still a few minutes away. Pascam Middle Grades stood on the city's edge in an abandoned warehouse, a fitting place to teach an abandoned and worthless skill set.

She stood near the tracks, staring into the dark tunnel. Part of her wished that it would stay empty. If only the train would break down so she could go home and say she had tried. A slight breeze skimmed across her face, and a low rumble echoed out of the tunnel. Her wish, like many others, would not come true. The train arrived. Its doors slid open with a whisper.

The car was mostly empty; Opal sat near the doors and looked around. A few other kids sat scattered throughout the car. She wondered if they were headed to Pascam too, or lucky enough to be going elsewhere. She shifted her backpack off her shoulder and placed it beside her.

A kid carrying a sticker-covered rollerboard got out at the next stop, hocking a big wad of spit onto the floor just as a thin, automated voice chimed over the speakers, "Please refrain from polluting or littering on the trains." Opal wished she could go rolling with him. The doors whooshed shut, and the train slid forward.

Across from her sat a boy in denims, wearing a flowing shirt with overlapping panels, and a vest in the Aelliven style. He was picking at his fingernails, head bowed, feet and knees pressed tightly together. Opal watched from the corner of her eye. She thought he might be whispering to himself. She leaned back, trying to seem uninterested.

As if he could feel her attention, the boy lifted his head and smiled at her, a knowing, almost smug smile. His eyes were nearly black beneath thick bangs. Opal pressed her lips into a half-hearted smile and looked away. She didn't want to encourage him. She didn't know why, but something about him creeped her out.

Her mood didn't improve once she got to Pascam Middle Grades of Magical Studies. At least her early classes were normal: Andrin History, Biology, Composition, and Sociology. Occasionally, she noticed the weird boy from the train sitting quietly in the back of her classroom, but he never spoke to her.

She kept to herself most of the day, even at lunch, not wanting to make friends. She still hoped she wouldn't be staying.

Finally, she reached the class she'd been dreading all day – Arcane Languages.

All castings were done in ancient Maellogi, which no one spoke anymore. The power had left the language or maybe it had left the people. Either way, here she was, spending her afternoon with a dead language, pretending that speaking it could do anything at all.

Instructor Miller, with tiny glasses and slicked-back gray hair, droned on about the old languages. Her eyelids drooped. She heard him call out her name, and was instantly awake. The instructor had picked her to read a casting. Her heart thudded hard against her ribs. Her stomach twisted.

She stood and walked to the front of the room where he motioned toward a massive, leather-bound book that had raised a cloud of dust when he dropped it on his desk.

"Open the Maellogic Tome," he said.

Opal flipped through stiff, dry pages and stopped on one filled with crude slashes and strange words.

"Can you read it?"

Maellogi used the same alphabet as her native Andrin. She couldn't understand the meaning, but she could sound out the words. She nodded.

"Very good. You've landed on Drawing a Karuk from the Lowest Realms. Please read it aloud."

Her thoughts raced. Bedtime stories were full of fools who summoned a karuk, thinking they could control it. Karuks were pure negativity. Even though the summoner had the power to banish the creature, their arrogance always got in the way. And what was more arrogant than a child summoning a karuk?

"But what if... ?"

Instructor Miller chuckled. "My, my. Were you not listening earlier? The words have no power. The mage provides the energy. Do you truly believe you have the power to bring a dark spirit into this world when no one has done it in centuries?"

The class erupted in laughter. Opal's cheeks burned.

"N-n-no."

"Then proceed with the reading."

She stared at the page, focused.

"Pesua delo mana . . ."

The air crackled.

". . . alie da fremila . . ."

The crackling became a sizzle. Opal glanced around, but no one seemed to notice. She kept reading. At first, the strange words stumbled from her mouth. Then, they began to flow. A buzzing rose around her. Her hair stood on end.

For the first time, Instructor Miller looked worried. She tried to stop reading, but couldn't. Anger at the whole situation bubbled out of her along with the final words of the casting. "Craci traos vellumnia adori sklica Biriad."

A roar like an airship engine filled the room. Thunder cracked, sounding as if the fabric of the universe was being ripped open. Opal flew backward, slamming into the wallscreen.

Then, silence. Blackness swallowed everything.

For a moment, Opal thought she might be dead. She reached toward Instructor Miller and instead touched something both freezing cold and burning hot, the Maellogic Tome.

Then she saw it. The creature.

Pupils glowing like embers, pulsing red to black. A jagged row of short horns jutted from its brow. Thick black hair bristled down its back. A long, thin nose sliced between sharp cheekbones, pointing to a grin filled with needle-sharp teeth... a smile that reeked of evil.

Everything else was gone: the desks, the tome, the teacher, her classmates. Only the grinning face of evil she had brought into the classroom remained.

"Thank you, child," it growled. Its voice made her bones vibrate.

The monster leaned closer, closed its eyes, and inhaled.

"Delicious," it whispered.

With a crack like thunder, the creature vanished. The blackness peeled away. Light returned.

Her classmates peeked over the tops of their desks from where they'd taken cover. Only the boy from the train hadn't moved. His dark eyes watched her, calm and wide, not afraid, but admiring.

She turned. Instructor Miller was crouching under his desk. When they made eye contact, he cleared his throat and croaked.

"Opal Hart, report immediately to the principal's office."

2

SOMETHING WICKED, SOMETHING WEAK

O ut of the nothing, Biriad heard his name called and, with a
delightful sharp pain, found himself inside a bright room full
of children. He felt unstable, as if a gust of wind could scatter him into
nothingness.

Nothingness was where he had come from. Utter darkness. Complete silence. Not a breeze touching his scaly skin. No landmarks. No
time. Each moment was an eternity, filled with terror and evil thoughts.
It had been unending misery.

He would not go back.

But why had he been brought into this plane?

He stared at the blonde-haired, blue-eyed girl standing before him.
Her terror was delightful. Though she was small and weak, he had to
get as far away as possible before she turned the page to read the casting
that would bind him to her.

He flew from the classroom and moved through the city, sliding
into shadows. He gaped at the towering buildings, each one offering countless dark places to hide. He stared, astonished, at the silent
carts enclosed in armor moving without horses. And there were so
many humans, all hurrying from place to place. Lights and pictures
flashed across some sort of massive windows. Machinery clattered and
hummed. Clearly, they had gained knowledge.

But he could see they had also become soft.

So much had changed. How long had it been since he last walked this realm?

He passed beneath a flickering sign, invisible under its neon glare. He found his first meal in a damp alley, thick with the reek of rotting vegetables. A man with greasy hair and stained coveralls moved stacked cases of produce from a large, covered cart into the back of a store. Biriad skimmed along the brick wall, his presence barely a shimmer.

The grocer noticed something move in the shadows. He wiped his hands on his overalls and stepped away from the truck, peering into the alley.

Biriad leapt.

He engulfed the man in one fluid motion. The grocer thrashed, clawing at empty air.

Warmth surged into Biriad's empty form as he watched the light fade from the man's eyes. But he was still weak. The man's life was no more than a mouthful of water to one who had been stranded in the desert. Delicious, but it didn't quench Biriad's burning thirst.

The grocer's body slid to the ground, an empty shell. Biriad looked at him without remorse. If anything, he felt satisfaction. Without him, this weak thing would have wasted the gift of existence on a simple, meaningless life. He had given the man's life a greater purpose.

Feeling more solid, Biriad lifted his hand and saw greenish-brown skin covered his ancient flesh. His long black claws gleamed. He raked his hand across the wall. He felt the scrape of brick, but still, his hand passed right through. He needed more food.

Last time, he'd re-formed quickly by feeding on primal wolves. Their dying fear and rage had made him powerful. But here there were no primal wolves. No dragons. Only humans, pale imitations of the creatures they'd once been. Magic no longer flowed through them. To return to full strength, he'd need a dozen lives. Maybe more.

He crept toward the street, but the glaring sun made his dark form too visible. He shrank back, hugged the wall, and used a dumpster as cover.

Not that anyone was paying attention. The river of humans passed by, heads bowed to glowing rectangles strapped to their wrists.

A young woman stepped out of the flow and into the alley, stopping just a few feet away. She was holding a board in front of her, speaking to a face flickering on its surface.

Biriad tilted his head. Magic may not flow through them, but they had learned to trap it in their machines.

She was completely distracted. The karuk saw his chance.

The woman's comscreen flew from her hands as he pulled her behind the dumpster. The fire of her youth surged into him. When he bumped up against the metal bin, he was solid enough that it rolled away at his touch.

He chuckled. He stretched his arms and chest. It felt good to be solid.

A shriek pierced the air. A woman on the street had seen the girl's foot poking out from behind the dumpster, and then she'd seen him.

The scream turned other heads. Everyone saw the karuk and began to shout.

Biriad grabbed a window ledge and effortlessly swung up four stories in a blink, then looked down from the roof at the crowd below.

A few of the City Guard arrived.

It amazed and amused him that they had no real weapons, only metal sticks. He reared back and let out a bellow. It was deep enough to shake the concrete. High enough to stab through eardrums.

For a few seconds, there was stunned silence. Then, the people turned and fled, everyone except the Guard.

Biriad was surprised when their sticks shot fire that struck his shoulder, making it burn with pain.

He loped across the roof, away from their weapons. Crouched against the far wall, he touched the wound. The strange fire had scorched his flesh, but it wasn't deep.

He needed to feed again, fast, to heal and continue gaining strength.

For the first time, he felt a flicker of worry. These creatures were weak, but their magical tools... their tools could hurt him.

He had to find the heart of their infestation, and exterminate them.

He crept to the rooftop's edge. More Guards were running toward the building. His eyes followed them, like watching a trail of ants, tracking them to their nest.

Biriad sprang from the shadows with new purpose, lunging across rooftops toward the King's Hall.

3

ECHOES IN THE STONE

Flint sat cross-legged on his cot, watching the video screen embedded in the wall of his dungeon cell buried deep under the King's Hall. He looked past the image, catching his reflection, hair smoothed back, mostly dark, but streaked with creeping gray. Pale skin from decades indoors, paired with his dark eyes, gave the illusion of a skull gazing back at him.

He sighed. It irritated him that inmates of the Magical Suppression Unit couldn't even use control gloves. The signal-dampening fields made them worthless. It was just one more thing to be angry about.

Flint stood, walked three steps to cross his cell, and turned on the screen. He flipped through the handful of programs available in the New Andrin dungeon: learn to make muffel casserole, knit a drago jacket, or suffer through amateur re-enactments of classic battles on the Andrin History Channel. The lack of anything remotely entertaining made him angrier than it should have.

He scanned the scenic channels until a golden wheat field appeared, snow-capped mountains in the distance. The wind rippling through the stalks reminded him of home. It helped him forget the bare cement walls of his twelve-by-ten-foot cell. Bed, desk, toilet, personal stash, that was his world.

He returned to his bed and stared at the screen, pretending he was a child again, looking out his bedroom window.

For a moment, the illusion held.

Then, like fog creeping in at the corners, came the metal bars. Came the sound of his fellow inmates, rotting away with him, their own vidscreens flickering. Reality pressed back in. Flint had led most of them here.

In the next cell over, out of view, was the man they called Goat. Bushy brown hair, squinty black eyes, and large chin covered in a wiry beard. The nickname fit. Like Flint, Goat would probably die down here. His power of invisibility made him especially dangerous.

Even though the magical dampening field kept him visible, the walls blocked Flint from seeing him. They could only talk.

"Hey, Goat," Flint called. "Remember when we brought that elevated train down during rush hour?"

"Sure do."

"Remember how good that felt?"

"Like scratching a bovila bite, fantastic, then the itch comes back twice as bad."

"Do you regret it?" Flint asked.

"Running it off the tracks? No. Why?"

"Just thinking about what could have kept us out of here."

Goat was quiet for a moment. Then he said, "If there's anything to regret, I suppose it was the airship collision. Though watching all those Drin falling from the sky was pretty fun."

"Yeah, I really thought they'd back off then. Never thought they had a way to stop us."

"Filthy Cavrek and their anti-magic tech," Goat muttered. He spat the name like a curse.

Flint smirked. Goat's short, stocky size meant he likely had Cavrek blood somewhere in his family.

The smirk faded as the room tilted. The walls seemed to spin. He grabbed the edge of his bed to keep from falling. The sensation passed almost as quickly as it came.

"You feel that, Goat?"

"What?"

"Nothing."

"You felt something. What was it?"

Flint paced. The cursed dampening field blocked his power, kept him from sending or receiving anything directly. But vibrations? He could still feel those. Something big had just moved through the city's magical threads.

He sat down and closed his eyes. He needed to focus.

Goat's voice, true to his name, bleated from the other cell. "C'mon Flint, what did you feel?"

Flint gritted his teeth. "Shut up!" he snapped.

Goat knew his boss well enough to obey.

Silence returned. Something powerful had stirred, too far away to reach, too significant to ignore. He couldn't connect to it. But he could become visible.

He pulled in what little energy he could from this void of a place, filling himself like a vessel in hopes something, someone, might see it from the outside.

Would it kill him? Save him? Ignore him?

After decades behind these walls, he didn't care anymore.

"Come and get me," he whispered.

4

THE GIRL WHO READ THE WORDS

Agent Bowman thumbed through the files on the compad in front of him as he waited for the meeting to begin. He pulled up Ben Hart's file and compared the picture of the pimple-faced teenager to the middle-aged man seated across the table. Oddly, they didn't look that different.

Ben was Opal's father and had also attended Pascam. His early test scores made the newly established school believe they had found their first protégé. But his failure to show any real talent after enrollment meant he was quietly transferred into Barker's Upper Grades of General Education. From what Bowman could tell, Ben had never developed any useful skills for the modern, technological world. He belonged to another time. He was arcane.

Superintendent Waters opened the meeting.

"We'd like to welcome Agent Bowman of the Department of Magical Defense. And of course, you all know Kingdom Administrator Steele."

That's how Agent Bowman knew things were serious. The kingdom administrator was the king's right-hand man.

"Thank you all for being here," the superintendent continued. "As some of you know, we had an unfortunate incident at the school this morning. Instructor Miller, please tell us what happened in your classroom."

Sweat beaded on Instructor Miller's temples. He twisted his hands.

"I'm not exactly sure. Every semester I start class the same way. I have one of the kids read a casting. This gives them a feel for the language, and helps them see the words don't actually do anything. I've never worried about which casting they choose. Generally they find a love or rain casting. Once it was the taming of a wild chicken. In twenty years, no student has ever caused even a ripple with a casting. Nothing. Then she picks that one."

Agent Bowman leaned forward, his pale gray eyes drilling into the teacher.

"Are you saying the girl chose the casting deliberately?"

"I had her open the book and read from the page it fell on. She had no idea what she was reading."

"You're sure?"

"They never do."

Ben erupted, "What casting did my daughter read? What could possibly have happened?"

Superintendent Waters raised a hand. "I know you're worried, but please bear with us... uh..." he glanced at the comtab. "What is your professional title?"

Ben lifted his chin, trying to appear confident. "I don't have one. You can call me Ben."

The superintendent continued, "Ben, we need your patience. Let's get through the facts first. Continue, Instructor Miller."

"She opened the page to Drawing a Dark Spirit from the Lower Realms. It is a high-level casting, yes, but I wasn't worried. No Drin alive has the power to make it work. She might as well have been reciting gibberish. I didn't think precautions were necessary."

"Obviously, that turned out to be false," Superintendent Waters said.

Instructor Miller shifted uncomfortably.

"In the future, it may be wise to take more control over which castings are read. What happened next."

"At first, her pronunciation was clumsy. Then it was like she'd been speaking Maellogi her whole life. The floor shook. Everything went black. There was a roaring sound, like a tornado. After a few minutes, everything went back to normal."

Agent Bowman narrowed his eyes. A girl who could cast without training? That kind of raw talent didn't stay hidden easily. "Ben, have you ever seen any sign your daughter had this sort of magical ability? Anything unusual at home?"

"Absolutely not. She's never shown the slightest interest in magic. She spends most of her time studying math and learning about space."

Superintendent Waters swiped her comtab.

"Ben Hart, you were a student here. You tested quite high in magical ability. Is that correct?"

"Yes, it is."

"Did you use your ability to teach Opal?"

"I have no magical ability. They mainstreamed me out of Pascam."

"Let's stay focused," Kingdom Administrator Steele cut in. "How the girl came by this ability doesn't matter. What matters is whether she can banish what she unleashed, and if her power can be controlled."

"Hold on," Ben said, "We don't even know that Opal summoned anything."

The room fell silent. Eyes darted away. Steele's expression darkened.

"I'm sorry to inform you," he finally said, "but your daughter did summon something. Something dark and very powerful. Shortly after the classroom incident, a karuk entered the King's Hall and killed the Guard and several ministers, good friends, right in front of me. There's no doubt it was the creature she called."

"How could that be possible?" Ben said. "She's never done a casting in her life. She didn't even know what she was reading. It's not her fault."

"Fault is not the issue. The real question is what happens next. If she can banish the karuk, what then? She may be the most powerful mage in generations. She could be an incredible asset to the kingdom."

"Or a terrible danger," a woman said. "There is no one qualified to teach her. If she stays untrained, she could become another Flint. We need to take custody of her."

"I think she should be studied," a man added. "We still don't understand where magic comes from. Maybe this girl is the key. Get her in a lab. Test her. Perhaps her father, too."

Ben's rose from his chair. "Opal is not going to a lab, and neither am I."

The room erupted. Voices swelled in overlapping waves of shouting, accusations, and fear.

No one seemed to remember the frightened girl waiting just outside the door - alone and terrified.

5

THE ESCAPE

Will stood outside the door to the administrative offices of the school. He was already breaking the rules by staying after everyone had been sent home. But he needed to find the girl who had summoned a karuk right in front of him. She'd been in his dreams that morning, and now he knew what the dream was telling him to do. He needed to help her escape.

He wanted to fling the doors open and charge in, but he had no idea where Opal might be or who might be waiting on the other side. Instead, he pushed the door open just a crack and couldn't believe his luck. Opal sat on the wooden bench outside a conference room, hugging her backpack to her chest. She was alone.

Will stepped inside quietly and sat at the far end of the bench. There was an awkward silence. Then he said, "Hi."

"Hi," Opal answered. "Did you get in trouble, too?"

"No."

They looked at each other, guarded.

"I'm Will."

"Opal. Will is a funny name."

"I'm named after Willin the Great."

"Oh."

They both stared ahead. The silence stretched.

"That was so cool," he said.

Opal turned to him. "What was?"

"Summoning that karuk."

"That was not cool. That was awful. How come you didn't hide like everyone else? Why were you so calm?" she asked.

"I wasn't," he said. "But it was amazing. I had to see what happened. Why are you here? Are they going to punish you?"

"I hope so. I hope they throw me out of Pascam."

Will blinked. He hadn't expected that. "Why? Where would you go to school then?"

"Deullen School of Science for Middle Grades, then Flomer School of Physics for Upper Grades. Then I'd get a degree in Physics from Kingdom University, and finally, I'd be in the space program."

"So why are you here?"

"Because even though my math scores were the highest of anyone in New Andrin, I tested even higher in magic, and my dad didn't even argue with the placement board. They usually let students go where they want, but this time, they didn't. And he let them. Coming here is so dumb."

"I don't think it's dumb at all. I wish I could do magic like you do."

Opal gave a short snort. "Magic is dumb."

Will dropped his eyes and picked at his thumbnail.

"I love magic," he said softly. Then he leaned in, voice low. "Opal, you need to come with me. Now."

She looked at him, startled. "What? Why?"

"I'll explain later. But we have to go before they decide something you can't undo. Trust me."

She hesitated, eyes narrowing.

Inside the conference room, the voices rose, but the words were muffled. Opal and Will moved to the door and pressed their ears against it.

Will and Opal's eyes widened as the adults talked about locking her up in a lab. If that happened, she'd never go into space. Never walk on the surface of another world. Never build a station or run experiments. Her future was collapsing.

She thought about running home, but that would be the first place they'd look. And then what? Dragged out in front of neighbors? Hauled away like a criminal? Her chest tightened. There was nowhere left to turn.

Tears blurred her vision.

Then - silence. The shouting in the conference room stopped.

The silence was worse.

Will reached out and grabbed her hand. His grip was firmer than she expected. He didn't look scared, but his clammy palm told a different story. "I can help," he whispered. "Come with me."

She stared at the weird boy from the train. His eyes were dark, unreadable, but something about them made her feel off-balance. "Where?" she asked.

"Please. Unless you've got a casting that freezes time, we've really got to go now. If they take you to a lab, you'll disappear. Nobody will stop the karuk. I know someone who can help you, I swear."

Opal looked at the door. Her dad was on the other side. She wanted to run to him. To say she was sorry. To feel safe. But then she heard the scrape of chairs. The meeting was ending.

Will's eyes pleaded with her. Decide. Now.

Images hit her in flashes: cold exam tables. Wires. Needles. Loneliness. And worse. What if they locked her away like Flint? At least with Will, she might still have a choice.

He tugged her hand gently. Her chest hitched with a breath, and she nodded.

They ran.

Her backpack thudded with every stride as they bolted down the empty hallway. Their footsteps echoed as they headed for the front door.

At the main doors, they hesitated. It was almost too easy.

A guard rounded the corner. "Hey! Stop!"

Will shoved the door open. Sunlight exploded around them. Opal stumbled but quickly caught her balance, and picked up speed. Voices shouted behind them. One sounded like her father. She didn't dare look back.

They sprinted through one twisting, narrow alley after another. One final turn and they burst onto Barkers Avenue swallowed by the crowd. They pressed against the side of a building, gasping for breath.

Will scanned the street.

"What are you looking for?" Opal asked, panting.

"Security cameras."

"There." She pointed across the street to a posh storefront.

"Nice. That one's not aimed at us. But that one," he nodded to a smaller pole-mounted unit, "we can't avoid. Keep your face down."

A rising siren screamed from somewhere up the street.

Will yanked them into the shadows, pressing their backs to the wall. He held his breath as the Guard's patroller shot past the alley, red and white lights strobing across the bricks. Only when the sound began to fade did he exhale.

"Where are we going?" Opal whispered, her voice sharp with panic.

Will's breath still caught at the edges, but he kept his voice steady. "Two blocks up. There's another alley network we can use."

"That's not what I asked."

"You'll see."

Will tapped his wristcom and brought it to life. "Keep your head down. Pretend we're looking at the screen."

They walked like any other teens killing time. But Opal expected to be grabbed, tackled, vanish in a blink.

"Where are we?" she asked. "How do you know your way around like this?"

"When I was little, I'd sneak out and play in these alleys. Pretend they were a maze. I'd rescue my parents from an evil overlord and fight my way to the castle."

"Seems kind of scary for a little kid."

"Nah. It kept me busy while my dad worked. He gets lost in his books. As long as I got home before the overlord finished his casting, which meant before my father noticed, I was fine."

He smiled faintly at the memory.

Will stopped abruptly; Opal stumbled into him.

"Shoo!" he shouted.

Opal flinched, but she soon realized he wasn't talking to her. Up ahead, a small cluster of dragos were digging through the trash. Once prized as exotic pets, the miniature dragons had become a citywide nuisance. They were expensive to feed and impossible to train. The rescues were full, so people just let them loose. Now they filled the city's alleys, scrounging for food and leaving drago droppings on the sidewalk. No wonder the alley stunk.

The dragos looked up but didn't fly away. Will yelled louder.

"Shoo!"

This time, most scattered, but one stood its ground. Opal had never seen a drago like it. It had dark red scales that turned black at the joints. Sleek. Beautiful. Wild. As it stared at them, the horns that ran from the back of its head to its tail rose in defense. It hissed. For a second, Opal worried it might have the ability to breathe fire, but it only launched upward, wings slicing the air as it landed on a fire escape above them, watching.

"Rats with scales and wings," Will muttered. "That's what my dad calls them. Fitting, right? Let's go."

"Go where?"

"This is where my dad works. We're at the back of Andrin Castle."

They looked up. Stone walls towered over them with small windows and arrow slits scattered across it. The ancient wall looked out of place directly across the alley from the back of a steel and glass office building.

Will jumped into a window well and pushed. The window held, then swung inward with a creak.

"A basement window in a castle? That seems weird," Opal said.

"It used to be a ramp for coal, wood, supplies, that sort of thing. It wasn't needed once the castle became a museum and was modernized. So, they put in a window. I've been using it to get in and out for years. Nobody bothers to check it."

While he worked at propping open the window, Opal looked up at the drago still watching them. She pulled an apple from her backpack, and set it on the street before jumping down next to Will.

With the window open, he grasped her hand and helped lower her into the room then dropped beside her. It took a moment for her eyes to adjust. Shapes loomed around them, vague and hulking.

"Do you have an e-torch?" Opal asked.

"I don't want to use it," Will said. "We might be seen."

She gripped the back of his shirt, using it as a guide as he shuffled forward.

Thud.

"Ouch!" Will hissed.

"You okay?"

"Fine. Just look out for the... " Will warned.

Thud.

Opal's shin collided with a wooden box. "Ouch! Look out for the crate?"

Will reached a door, eased it open a crack, and listened. Then he waved her through.

They crept along ancient, dimly lit corridors. The stone walls were old, the air cool and slightly damp. Will pulled her into a dark opening, to a winding stone staircase.

"This is so cool!" Opal whispered as they climbed. Her fingers brushing the stone as they climbed. "Do you think King Cormer the Third ever touched these walls?"

"If you like this, wait until you see where we're going. The tower room where Lady Angeluna went mad."

"Awesome!"

"Unless she visits."

"Her ghost actually haunts it?"

Will shrugged. "I've never seen her. Once I smelled perfume and felt a hand in my hair, but there were flowers under the window, and a breeze. Could've been nothing."

The stairs ended at a heavy wooden door. It took all Will's strength and weight to pull it open enough for them to squeeze through.

"Wait here," he whispered.

"Seriously? Alone?"

"I'll just be a minute. You'll be fine."

He disappeared inside.

Opal stood in the dark, fighting off every image her imagination conjured. Ghosts. Chains. Screams. Instead, she focused on roast beef. And mustard. And warm bread.

"It's safe. Come on in," Will said.

Opal stepped through, and forgot all about the sandwich.

The tower room was frozen in time. Dust-laced light funneled through a narrow window, illuminating a bed with a carved headboard and faded canopy. An old rocker sat by the cold fireplace. Logs still waited in the grate, like they expected someone to return.

Opal could almost see Lady Angeluna there, rocking slowly, whispering secrets to the fire.

A wardrobe gaped open, its only occupants cobwebs and dust.

"This is amazing," she breathed. "Why doesn't anyone come up here?"

"They used to. It was probably one of the most popular stops of the tour. Then some idiot shouted 'fire' at the bottom of the stairs. People panicked. Two died. Without two exits, Public Safety shut it down."

She turned towards him. "So, what now? Are we just going to live here forever?"

"Of course not. My father likes to stay late and work when nobody's around. We'll wait until the museum closes and then go find him. He'll know what to do."

Opal looked at him skeptically as she removed her backpack and let it drop to the floor.

"He will," he assured her.

She wanted to believe him. Because she had no plan. No options. And it felt like the whole world was hunting her.

6

THE ENTIRE DEPARTMENT

Agent Gale Bowman sat at his desk staring at his comscreen. He had hit replay dozens of times and still wasn't sure if he'd seen the kids. If it was them, they might be heading toward Andrin Castle. He'd already spoken to the boy's father, and his gut said the man had told the truth: Will and Opal weren't at the museum.

The logicomp rang.

Emergency Management Deputy Chief Tanner's stern face appeared on the screen. Her close-cropped silver hair, high cheekbones, and emotionless eyes gave her an intimidating edge, one she clearly knew how to use.

"Hello, Deputy Chief. How can I help you?"

"Tell me you've found them."

"I'm sorry, I haven't. They're... Well, they seem to be avoiding security cameras. It's like they've vanished."

"It seems unlikely children could avoid capture, unless the person searching for them is incompetent."

Tanner let the silence stretch, pressing him under the weight of her stare.

"For years I've diverted money from preparing for actual natural disasters to keep your department alive. The old geezers on the Council might love their magical fairy tales, but you're a drain on this kingdom. Maybe the real disaster was trusting you. And now your little prodigy has blood on her hands. Bring her in. Stop this before anyone else gets hurt. Do you understand?"

She didn't wait for an answer. With a flick of her wrist, the video call went dead.

He clenched his jaw. He'd outlasted six directors and three funding cuts. He could outlast her too, if this mess didn't finish him first.

He looked around his office. There was just a desk, a flickering screen, and a stack of unanswered reports. He liked telling people he was with the Department of Magical Defense, but the truth was, he was the department. Once there were colleagues, a secretary, even a coffee machine. Now, it was just him, and the cold hum of a job no one believed in.

The council's oldest members had fought to keep the department funded, the budget had been whittled back year after year. If Bowman couldn't fix this mess, he'd be out of a job.

He flipped open Opal Hart's file again, remembering how the hairs on the back of his neck had stood when he'd first saw her aptitude test scores. The highest he'd ever seen. He'd personally overseen the retesting. No doubt, she had real power.

Her mother's side had produced mages four or five generations back but nothing recent. Instead, the past few generations had been exceptionally talented in math and science. Her mother had worked as a scientist for the Kingdom until she died in a lab explosion. That explained Opal's exceptional science scores.

But the magic? That likely came from her father. He also had a great deal of power, but his records showed no aptitude during school. When placing Opal, Bowman had worried she'd be another spectacular failure, like her dad.

This morning had ended that worry.

Now the question was: what to do with her?

No living Drin could teach a mage with this kind of power. Maybe she could learn the basics, read through the archived diaries of the great mages stored in the basement, but wisdom didn't come from dusty pages. She needed more than theory.

The only option was the Aellivi.

And that would be a hard sell. The small folk knew their fate was intertwined with the rest of the human race, but since the Great Kingdom Wars, they kept their distance. There was much distrust; Bowman wasn't sure they'd agree to teach a Drin girl.

Funny. A betrayal thousands of years ago might now doom them all.

He closed the folder with a sigh. It wouldn't matter what the Aellivi could offer if Opal wasn't in custody. Only the summoner could banish a karuk. Bowman would try to get a message to his old friend Roa, who might convince the Aelliven council to help.

It was the best Bowman could do.

And judging by the growing body count, it wouldn't be nearly enough.

7

THE DOOR AND THE DEAL

Biriad had followed the Guard to their barracks and consumed the lives of the entire group. Now at full strength for the first time in millennia, he killed purely for enjoyment. From the barracks, he continued into the adjoining King's Hall, a gleaming modern structure with polished floors and bright hallways. There, he discovered a cluster of soft, plump government leaders. Their terror was exceptionally delicious.

Suddenly, he felt it. Power. A force pulling at him like iron to a magnet. He couldn't resist. Disoriented, he hurled himself down a stairwell, leaping from landing to landing into the depths of the complex.

***

On the lowest level, Cooper, a nineteen-year-old rookie guard, had pulled dungeon duty for oversleeping his patrol. It was the most boring post imaginable. No action. No danger. For the past hour, he'd been mentally replaying the thirty-seventh level of WarMongers. Every time he sent a wedge of mage archers to flank the Repticin foot soldiers, primal wolves wrecked his main line. He'd tried different forces and angles but could never get past that level. No matter the strategy, he couldn't break through. He was starting to consider a cheat code, though he hated cheating. What was the point of playing if you let someone else solve it for you?

The far door burst open.

Something stepped through, something far worse than anything Cooper had ever seen on his screen. Black-haired legs ending in massive lupine paws. A muscular chest with scaly greenish-brown skin. Arms like tree trunks. Long claws. And the face, a snarling, sharp-featured not quite human face - horror with jagged teeth and eyes that burned with something ancient and cruel.

Cooper slid along the wall, quivering, trying to melt into the surface. The monster's claws clicked closer on the sterile tile floor leading to the dungeon's main entrance.

"Open the door," it hissed.

Cooper froze. It spoke. And in Andrin.

The monster loomed at least seven feet tall over him. It bent over to peer directly into his eyes.

"Open the door. NOW!"

Cooper's bladder let go. He collapsed, trembling, then crawled to the security panel and punched in the code. If he survived, he might be court-martialed, but he didn't care. He'd find another career. Something without monsters.

The door slid open.

Cooper closed his eyes and waited for the fatal blow.

When nothing came, he peeked, just in time to see the creature vanish through the door.

He ran for the lifter.

***

Biriad entered the dungeon. A narrow hallway stretched before him, lined with concrete cells and iron bars. Prisoners cowered as he passed.

At the end of the hall was the cell that had drawn him. It held a man unlike the others. He stood calmly. He didn't flinch. He didn't shrink. He smiled, though his eyes betrayed the fear that Biriad brought with him.

He was tall for a Drin, about six-and-a-half feet. Dark hair flecked with gray hung past his collar. His eyes were alert, calculating. The crow's feet formed by his smile showed him to be in his mid-fifties.

He and Biriad studied each other, unmoving.

Finally, the man spoke.

"Are you going to let me out?"

"Why should I?"

"Because I am the only person alive who doesn't want to kill you, Biriad. I never imagined you'd walk into my dungeon, but here you are. You are legend in my family. The documentary they showed us in school didn't do you justice."

The creature processed the strange words. He knew most, but some were new. Boots pounded above. More of the Guard were descending.

"My name is Flint," the man continued, glancing toward the noise. "I come from the line of Alberoth."

Biriad's attention sharpened at the name of his old ally.

"I drew you to me," Flint said quickly. "I have his power in me, perhaps more than he had. Together, we can defeat your summoner and keep you in this world. We can rule together. Alberoth lacked the vision. I don't."

The boots grew louder.

"Hurry! Hit the yellow pad on the wall. It controls the magic-dampening field. I'll do the rest."

Biriad hesitated. Alberoth had been a strong ally. But he'd been betrayed by him. Maybe this time, he'd write the rules. Burn the summoner. Burn them all.

"You have no other way out, Biriad. They can trap you in solid form. Only I can help."

With a snarl, Biriad tapped the glowing yellow pad with one vicious claw. The magic-dampening field let out a high-pitched buzz, then fell silent.

Flint's cell door slid open. For the first time in decades, he stepped free without manacles.

The Guard arrived outside the door.

He whispered a casting. Searing white light flew from his fingertips blasting the door with scorch marks.

The soldiers used a small battering ram, but it held.

Flint passed each cell, fingers grazing the bars, as if anointing the faithful. With every touch: a metallic click. A breathless silence. A door easing open.

One by one, prisoners stepped out. Some looked dazed. Others ready.

Stone, one of the petty thieves he'd mentored, remained in his cell, watching silently. Waves of defiance came off him, and Flint knew he would have to stop that immediately.

"You owe me," Flint said, voice low. "Some of you owe your power to me. All of you now owe me your freedom. I will call on you."

He turned slowly, meeting each set of eyes. "When I call, you will come. Or you'll learn that your freedom was just a pause before a painful death."

He walked to a nearby keypad, placed his hand on it, and spoke a casting. Sparks flew from the pad, swirling around his arm. The lights flickered as every prisoner vanished from the dungeon.

Flint turned to Biriad.

"Thank you, my friend. Now, let's find a safe place to discuss our alliance."

He placed a hand on Biriad's shoulder and whispered a longer incantation.

They vanished.

The dungeon was filled with the silence that comes before something much, much worse.

8

THE GHOST ROOM

Will and Opal sat in uneasy silence. The air in the old castle room was cool. The quiet was broken only by the distant murmur of city noise. Opal hugged her knees tighter, staring at nothing. The adrenaline had faded. Now all that remained was the weight of not knowing what would happen next.

Dust motes drifted in the amber light of the arrow slits. Will traced a finger through the dust on the floor. Opal began to relax in the stillness of the room. He drew marks on the floor. Xs and Os. She wasn't really up for a game but played along anyway.

As the day faded, they sat shoulder to shoulder on the cold stone floor, the weight of the day pressing in from all sides.

The courtyard erupted in a staccato burst of gunfire, making both of them jump. "That's the closing ceremony," Will said. "We should give it another hour. By then everyone will be gone, and we can find my father."

"Do you think he'd call my dad? Let him know I'm okay?"

"Probably. Where does your dad work?"

"He doesn't," Opal said, trying not to sound embarrassed. "He's too arcane, and all the menial jobs wouldn't pay enough to cover childcare for me, so we scrape by on my mom's Kingdom death benefits."

Will looked away, visibly uncomfortable. "I'm sorry."

"It's okay. My dad and I do alright. He can't always give me what I want, but he always has time for me." She smiled faintly. "One year, I begged and begged for a spacescope with gel lenses for my birthday. There was no way he could afford that, so he bought supplies and helped me build an old-school one with glass lenses. It's one of my favorite things."

"That's cool. Honestly? I'm a little jealous."

"Why?"

"I love my parents. They're great, but... They would've just bought me the spacescope and said, 'Have fun.' Dad's busy here. Pop is an artist and always at his gallery."

He laughed, a little embarrassed. "Last year they got me a flexiglass rollerboard with antigrav wheels. I don't even roll."

"Now I'm jealous. I love rolling. I have wanted one of those boards since they came out. All I have is my old plastic one, and I'm too embarrassed to take it to the roller park."

"You can have mine," Will said. "If you promise that when this is all over, I can come hang out with you and your dad."

"I promise."

Opal grinned and launched into stories from the roller park, close calls, cool tricks, and a spectacular wipeout, until the room was completely dark.

They eased the door open and crept down the winding stairway, Will in the lead. The hallways were dim and silent. Every shadow felt like a possible guard or lurking curator, but the museum was empty.

The last time Opal had been here, the place was packed. Her school group had shuffled past the exhibits while the teacher droned on from the front. She hadn't seen much of anything. But now, everything was visible. The kingdom's history surrounded her: the coronation robe and scepter, the table where the Peace Accord was signed.

She stopped short at a velvet-roped floor exhibit: a thick wooden block with a heavy axe leaning against it.

"Is that the actual executioner's block?" she whispered.

"It is."

"Can I touch it?"

"Go ahead. That darker stain is real soaked-in blood. It's not faked with paint."

Opal slipped under the rope. She pictured enemy kings and traitors kneeling here, waiting for the end. She imagined herself stepping forward, placing her neck in the hollow. How had those people not run? She reached out to touch the groove where so many lives had ended.

A door slammed in the distance.

Opal jumped back, heart pounding. Will motioned frantically, waving her into the shadows. She ducked under the rope and hurried to his side.

"It's probably my dad," he whispered. "Stay quiet, just in case."

They crept toward the noise. Soft yellow light spilled from one of the chambers.

"I think we're good. That's my dad's office."

They leaned cautiously into the doorway.

Will's father sat hunched over his desk. The ceiling lights were off, but a desk lamp cast a soft circle of light across his shoulders, and over a large sandwich cut in half on a plate next to him.

"Dad?" Will whispered.

The man jumped, knocking the sandwich to the floor. His thinning blond hair and closely trimmed beard caught the light.

"Will! Where have you been? There's a karuk loose in the city."

"I know. I've been helping Opal."

"But she's the one who..." He cut himself off, eyes locked on the girl behind Will. "There's a lot of people looking for you, young lady."

Will's father stopped and studied Opal. Feeling embarrassed by the scrutiny, she dropped her gaze to the sandwich on the floor, her stomach rumbling with hunger.

"I'm Doctor Weaver, Will's father," he said. "Why don't you tell me what happened... over some food?"

Both kids lit up.

Weaver led them through a narrow stone corridor to a kitchen that looked caught in a standoff between centuries. Sleek appliances sat shoulder-to-shoulder with cast-iron relics. Cooking tools dangled from a high rack above a slate table. The scent of bread hung faintly in the air.

He made quick sandwiches for the kids and a fresh one for himself. They tore into theirs, chewing before they even sat down.

When their plates were mostly crumbs, they began to talk, halting at first, then gaining momentum. Weaver listened, nodding occasionally, but said nothing. When Opal described how the government wanted to study her, his expression darkened.

He rose, pacing the tile in long, tight strides. His hands clenched behind his back.

"I think Opal is the girl Trellin's looking for," Will said.

His father turned to him and said, "That might make sense."

Opal leaned forward. "Who's Trellin?"

Doctor Weaver blinked, as if suddenly reminded she was still there. He sat down again.

"He's my third cousin. He secretly loans me Aelliven artifacts for the museum, items the Elders would never approve. In exchange, he asked me to keep an eye out for a girl with unusually strong magical ability."

Opal frowned. "Why would he want to know that?"

"I don't remember exactly. We'd both had too much Cavrek rum the night he told me. Something about a prophecy... or a hunch. It made sense at the time."

A cold prickling crept over Opal. Someone out there was looking for her. Shadows flickered at the edges of her vision, making her feel watched.

Everyone knew the Aellivi distrusted the Drin. Some believed the decline in magical ability was payback for Belken's betrayal. What if they weren't looking to help her at all?

"Or maybe they want to kill me," she muttered.

Doctor Weaver looked startled. "Why would they want to do that?"

"Because Belken proved the Drin are better mages," she said, defensively.

Doctor Weaver let out a short, dry laugh.

"Belken was a fraud. A braggart. And an absolute idiot."

Opal blinked. "He saved the Drin. His lies were justified."

"Saved them?" Weaver scoffed. "He nearly destroyed the Aellivi. And he shattered the trust between our peoples. That lie cost more than lives, it cost centuries of peace."

He stood again; voice tight with anger.

"What they don't teach you is that Belken cheated his way through school. His magical skills were barely passable. Most of his so-called feats were done by others, shadow casters hidden just out of sight. He mimicked their movements well enough to fool the teachers. That's how he rose to command."

Opal's throat tightened. She wasn't sure she wanted to hear the rest, but she didn't stop him.

"When Andrin faced destruction, Belken didn't have the power to save it. So, he manipulated our allies into fighting his battle. The Aellivi paid the price. Their people, their culture, their magic, nearly wiped out. It took them generations to recover. So no, Opal. That lie wasn't justified."

She sat quiet, thinking. "No wonder they hate us."

"They don't hate us," Doctor Weaver said, softer now. "But they don't trust us. And they have reason not to. My guess is Trellin wants to make sure someone like you doesn't repeat Belken's mistakes."

Will leaned forward. "Dad, you need to call him. See what he says."

Opal snorted. "Call him on what? The Aellivi don't use the InfoMax."

Everyone knew that. The Aellivi were famous for avoiding modern tech.

"They do so," Will replied. "They have a central terminal where you can leave a message."

"That's right, Opal," Doctor Weaver added. "The Aellivi figured out a long time ago that the best way to keep us out of their world is to let a little of ours in."

They returned to Doctor Weaver's office and left a short, carefully word-ed message for Trellin. The response came quickly. Doctor Weaver had been right, the Aellivi wanted Opal brought there immediately.

The next few hours passed in a flurry of planning, booking couriers, dis-guising the shipment, and arranging transport to the largest Drin city near the border. No one would question a crate from the Kingdom Museum headed for the West Doyova Museum of History.

When the final confirmation of the shipment beeped across the screen, Will's dad turned to Opal.

"Don't worry," he said. "I'll make sure you can breathe and have food and water in the crate."

"Will you let my dad know where I am?"

"It's safer if he doesn't know," Doctor Weaver said gently. "But I'll tell him you're safe once you've arrived in Aellivi."

Opal's throat tightened. She looked down at her hands, clenched in her lap.

"He won't sleep," she whispered. "He'll think something terrible hap-pened to me."

Doctor Weaver paused. "I know. I'm sorry."

Opal turned away, blinking fast. She didn't cry, not in front of strangers.

"I'm going too," Will announced.

"No. I can't let you do that," Doctor Weaver said.

"I have to," Will said, voice steady. "I helped Opal escape. If I stay, they'll arrest me. And besides..."

He hesitated, then looked at Opal.

"I dreamed her, Dad. Before all this happened. I think I was meant to help her."

Weaver stared at his son. Then, with a reluctant sigh, he nodded.

"Fine," he said. "We'll use a bigger crate."

9

ABOVE IT ALL

Will lay slumped on top of packing blankets inside the crate, sound asleep in the airship's cargo bay. Above them, two window seats awaited, but it would be a while before their contact could let them out. Opal sat beside him, knees drawn to her chest, but her thoughts were already floating elsewhere.

Airships.

She had read every book the library had on them: technical manuals, history texts, even one illustrated guide clearly meant for younger kids. It didn't matter. She'd devoured them all.

The earliest fliers had used dragons. Mages could sometimes control them with harnesses and castings, but they were unpredictable, wild, and difficult to manage. Worse, they couldn't carry much. However, their legacy lived on in gas.

Years ago, daring Cavrek scientists had stolen several dragon eggs from Vulkera Island in the Southern Ocean. They wanted to understand how creatures that massive could fly, and what powered their legendary fire. Surprisingly, both questions had the same answer.

Dragons created a gas inside their bodies, lighter than air and highly flammable. This gas filled their bodies, making them much lighter than they appeared and allowing them to get into the air. It also allowed them to breathe fire. It collected in a chest sac that emptied into the lungs, and was sparked into flame by their back teeth, like steel against flint.

Some scientists bred smaller versions domesticated as household pets called dragos. Through breeding, they were able to remove the flammable nature of the gas the dragos produced, thus taking away their fire breathing ability. Scientists called this new gas dragozo. Most kids called it drago farts. And drago farts made modern air travel possible.

Opal smiled at the thought. She was in an airship. Not watching from the terminal platform. Not seeing one from down on the street. She would be in the sky, even if she was locked in a crate. Still counted.

Outside this crate, the ship would be gleaming and massive. Shaped like a long, stretched-out egg, some were two city blocks long. Inside, there would be restaurants, couches, shops, and sunlit windows. The metal hull soaked up solar power, tanks filled with dragozo kept the ship afloat, and jet engines on long spindly wings would carry it forward.

And here she was, stuck inside a crate next to a sleeping boy, not able to see any of it.

Will jerked upright and shouted something unintelligible.

Opal clicked on the e-torch. His eyes were wide and glassy. His whole body had gone stiff, and his mouth was shaped into a perfect circle, as if caught mid-word.

"Will?" she shook his shoulder.

He blinked. His eyes focused. He was back.

"You alright?" she asked.

"Fine." He rubbed the back of his neck, ducking his head. "It was just a dream."

She remembered what he'd said to his dad. *I dreamed her.*

"What is the deal with you and dreams?"

He motioned for a water flask from the corner. Opal handed it to him. He drank slowly, like he was stalling.

Finally he spoke. "I guess I can tell you. Every morning, right before I wake up, I have a dream. But not like a normal dream. These are different. I call them true dreams. Weird things happen in them, but as the day goes on, I realize parts of it were real. If I pay attention, sometimes I can keep bad stuff from happening."

She raised her eyebrows.

"What did you dream about me?"

"You were holding a book. You and the book were glowing. Everything else was dark. Then a flash, and I saw Instructor Miller sending you to the principal's office. Then we were running"

"What did you dream about just now?"

"I don't like to say until after it happens."

The airship shuddered. A high-pitched whine rose and deepened into a roar.

"We're in the air," Opal whispered.

The muffled thrum of engines and the faint creaking of the ship could be heard, even in the crate.

"Would you tell me if you dreamed I was going to die?" she asked.

He glanced sideways at her. "It doesn't work like that. They're not... prophecies. More like clues. Sometimes I miss them completely."

"Does it ever tell you anything useful? Like what lottery numbers to play?"

A soft metallic clack echoed at the far end of the cargo bay. A door opened and shut.

They went quiet.

Footsteps, getting closer.

Then, a light tap on the crate.

"You two in there?" whispered a voice.

They both exhaled.

"Yes," Will replied, voice low.

Latches were unclipped. The crate's side folded down, spilling Opal onto the floor. She rolled over and stood, brushing herself off. Will grabbed his backpack, now filled with food, traveling supplies, and the small amount of cash his father had given him.

An older man stood in front of them with white hair and an unkempt beard, grinning. Short and wide, with pale blue eyes, he appeared to be half Cavrek and half Drin.

"You must be Jomin's boy, Will," he said. "It's a real pleasure to meet you and help you on your way. Your dad's helped me and mine more times than I can count. And you must be Opal. You can call me Avo."

He handed them each a thin plastic card.

"These are your airship passes. They'll get you into the passenger lounge and let you use the ship's services while you're aboard. When we arrive at West Doyova, you'll get off the ship with the rest of the passengers, unless we get word they're looking for you there. New Andrin has declared a state of emergency. It won't take long for emergency law to spread to other cities. If that happens, I'll come find you in the lounge and smuggle you out the way you came in."

"A state of emergency? We can't be that important," Opal said.

Avo's expression turned serious.

"I'm sorry, but you are. The karuk has killed people. They won't be able to stop it until they have you."

"We have to go back then," Opal said, her voice cracking.

"You can't," Avo said gently. "You have a better chance of stopping it with the Aellivi."

Tears gathered in Opal's eyes. "How many people has it killed?" she whispered.

"I don't know," Avo responded, his voice kind but heavy.

"What happens when we get off the airship? Where do we go?" Opal asked.

"Trellin will be waiting with the museum truck. He'll take care of you from there." He pointed to a door. "Now head through there and take the stairs up to the passenger lounge."

Opal wiped her eyes and took off toward the door, trying to put distance between herself and the knowledge she was responsible for people dying.

She stopped at a porthole to watch a giant tether being retracted into the ship's hull. This was the second stage of takeoff. The view from the lounge had to be incredible.

Will caught up with her in the passenger lounge, a massive, stadium-sized area with couches, tables, a food court, and shops. Concave windows, seats, and tables ringed the room.

Opal hadn't made it to their table. She stood in the center of the lounge, staring upward, transfixed. Will followed her gaze. All he saw was a series of supports in the massive airship ceiling.

"I wonder what Tias would think of this," she said softly. "She built the first airship in her barn, and it barely held her family."

"You mean the Flya from Castia?" Will wrinkled his nose. "We had to read about that in third year. Boring."

Will glanced at his ticket and started toward their table. Opal followed.

"Tias was not boring. She was a genius inventor. She taught herself engineering and started experimenting with dragozo in her barn. Everything we're seeing right now, started with her."

Will shrugged. "Whatever. Her first airship was basically a floating balloon on a rope. They sold tickets to ride up and down."

They found their seats, two plush chairs with a small table between them beside a large, curved window overlooking the port below.

"Yeah, but then she added wings and turbines," Opal said, settling into her seat.

"And she crashed," Will replied flatly. "What a genius."

"She was." Opal insisted. "Science is about failing until you succeed. Once she got out of the hospital, she redesigned the whole thing. She piloted her family from their farm in Castia to New Andrin in a record-breaking four hours."

Will leaned toward the window, more interested in the shrinking world below than history.

An announcement played from the speakers.

"Ladies and gentlemen, we have reached take-off altitude. Acceleration can be disorienting. For your safety, we ask that you take your seat until we reach cruising speed."

Opal leaned her forehead against the window, craning to see one of the massive wings. It held two jet engines. The turbines began to spin, and the airship surged forward. The land slid away below them. For a moment, the floor seemed to tilt under her, but her brain quickly adjusted to the speed.

Watching from the ground, Opal had often wondered about the people in departing airships. Where were they going? What were they thinking? What did they see? Now, she was one of them. The city that seemed so large on the ground shrank to the size of her old Tiny Town playset as they climbed upward. She tried to recognize buildings by their rooftops, but the view was so unfamiliar, it was impossible to be sure.

"Look, there's Pascam." Will said.

"Where?"

He pointed. Opal pressed her nose hard against the glass, spotting the campus on the city's edge. Tiny figures streamed toward the school from all directions. Just yesterday, she might have been one of them, dreading homework or wishing for someone to pull the fire alarm. Now she was on the run, hunted for something she didn't mean to do, carrying the weight of lives lost.

She longed to be one of those kids walking to class; secondhand clothes, bad haircut, and all. If someone gave her a time machine, she'd go back to yesterday and pick a different casting. She'd sit through class and actually pay attention. She'd be happy just to be a student again, even if it meant studying magic. Her chest tightened with longing.

New Andrin drifted away behind them, replaced by a quilt of fields and roads. They headed toward a bank of puffy white clouds. Opal was eager to see what it was like inside. From the ground, clouds looked like they had valleys and ridges hidden within them. But when they entered the vapor, the world turned to fog. She hadn't realized that clouds were just fog in the sky. Once the airship broke through the top, the clouds turned magical again, full of castles and cliffs.

Will and Opal spent time exploring the passenger lounge. It was like being in a flying mall. They returned to their seats when breakfast service began in their section.

A uniformed attendant stopped beside them.

"Good morning, young sir. Miss. Can I get you anything from the breakfast menu?"

"Eggs, bacon, and toast, please," Opal said quickly.

"And for you, sir?"

Will rested his chin on his hand, tapping the side of his mouth thoughtfully, as he studied the menutablet.

"I'll have . . . hmmm... Maybe . . . No wait. I know! Tokaberry waffles. Do you have those now?"

"You're in luck," the attendant said with a smile. "Tokaberries are in season. We just got a fresh batch."

"Thank you!"

"When do we reach full speed?" Opal asked, staring at the ground passing slowly beneath them.

"We already have," the attendant said. "Is this your first flight?"

Opal nodded, wide-eyed.

"You needn't be frightened," the attendant assured her, mistaking her awe for anxiety. "Where are your parents? Let's ask them if I can take you to meet the captain. That might make you feel better."

Opal froze. She wanted to visit the command center more than anything, but the last thing she needed was to draw attention to herself.

She spotted a couple across the lounge who looked vaguely parental.

"There they are," She waved at the couple, who stared at her without recognition.

"But don't bother them," Opal added quickly. "I'm not scared. It just seems like we're going really slow. I read that airships can go up to six hundred miles per hour."

"It may feel slow up here," the attendant said with a smile, "but we are cruising at approximately five hundred fifty miles per hour right now. Welcome to the clouds, young lady. I'll be right back with your breakfast."

"Have you ever had tokaberry waffles?" Will asked Opal once the attendant left.

"I've never had tokaberry anything. My dad always said it's environmentally wasteful to import them from the southern continent, but honestly, I think he just didn't want to admit we couldn't afford them."

"You can have some of mine," Will said. "They are so good. Once you taste them, you won't care how wasteful it is. You'll want them every day for the rest of your life."

When their food arrived, the attendant also brought Opal a cloud-shaped pin to wear on her shirt, a welcome token for her first airship trip. Opal felt him watching her carefully as she pinned it on. She hoped he hadn't talked to 'her parents' across the room. Nothing she could do about it now.

Will was right about the waffles. They practically dissolved on her tongue, leaving behind a single, round, hard tokaberry. She pressed it to the roof of her mouth until it burst. She'd never tasted anything like it. Tart and sweet, but with a strange effect. She felt the flavor throughout her body. Ordinary pancakes were officially over.

With her stomach full and clouds rolling below, Opal forgot everything: the chase, the deaths, the fear. She was flying, and the world was far away.

"In preparation for deceleration, we ask that you please take your seats," came the announcement. "We will notify you when we reach tethering speed. At that time you will be free to gather your belongings and make your way to the nearest disembarking ramp. Exit doors will open only after docking is complete and the ramps are secured. Please do not attempt to exit before the disembark sign is illuminated."

Opal blinked. The two-hour flight had flown by. Literally.

Will leaned back, let out a tiny burp, and grinned. "Excuse me."

Opal wrinkled her nose at first, but his impish grin made her laugh. She inhaled deeply and returned fire with a burp of her own.

Will snorted mid-laugh, which only made Opal laugh harder. A few nearby adults shot them disapproving looks. She didn't care. It felt good to laugh. It felt normal.

Their fun was cut short when Avo appeared beside them and tapped Will's shoulder.

"Come quickly," he said, voice low and urgent.

10

THE WEAK LINK

P ing!

The soft sound from the comscreen nudged Agent Bowman from a light sleep. His legs, resting on his desk, tingled with numbness. He swung them down and rolled forward, bringing the screen into focus. A red flag blinked next to Jomin Weaver's name. Bowman tapped the alert. A string of late-night calls and a shipping manifest popped up: one large crate to West Doyova.

A crate?

It had to be the kids. Weaver had lied to him.

Bowman rubbed his eyes and checked the time: two hours past dawn. He cursed under his breath and opened the New Andrin flight schedule. The airship was already in the sky.

If Deputy Chief Tanner found out he'd let them slip away, he was finished. At least they were still in the air. Maybe he could spin it, say he'd allowed them to flee because it would be easier to apprehend them on arrival. It was a weak move, but it might buy him time. He pulled up the comms interface and called West Doyova.

Chief Carter appeared, square jaw, piercing brown eyes, and a cloud of black curls. She looked alert, if a little confused.

"Chief Carter of the West Doyova Guard. How can I assist the Department of Magical Defense?"

"Have you been briefed on the situation in New Andrin?"

"Only what's made the news."

Bowman gave her the rundown in clipped sentences. She frowned as he spoke.

"Terrible, just terrible," she said. "Do you need reinforcements? We could send a regiment of Guard."

"That's generous. I'll pass your offer along. Right now, I need your people at the skyport. We believe the girl who summoned the karuk is aboard airship Voyix24, along with the boy who helped her escape. It's likely they stowed away in a crate. They may have slipped into the passenger lounge. I'm sending photos and a shipping manifest now."

He tapped furiously across his sensepad.

"Received," Carter said. She studied Opal's face. "She's young to have caused this much trouble. I'll forward these to the airship's security team."

"Warn them to be careful. The girl's powerful. She unleashed this thing accidentally. Imagine what she could do if she's provoked. And she's proven to be slippery."

"What about the boy? Is he dangerous?"

"Not really. He has some talent in precognition. Probably how they've stayed a step ahead."

"And if we catch him?"

"Send him back to his parents."

Carter tilted her head. "One moment. Their security officer is calling in. Let me add him to the call."

A second window opened. A young man, barely in his mid-twenties, appeared on-screen. His uniform was crisp, his posture stiff.

"Security Officer Hawk." The young man said, puffing out his chest.

Bowman raised an eyebrow. Perfect. A rookie.

"One of our attendants spoke with two kids matching the description," Hawk said. "They didn't seem to be with an adult."

A recorded voice played faintly behind him: "In preparation for deceleration we ask that you please take your seats . . ."

"You're landing?" Bowman snapped. "Why are you talking to me? Take them into custody now. Do not let them leave that ship. Lives depend on this."

Hawk paled. "Y-yes, sir."

His screen went black.

"Send your Guard to the ramps," Bowman told Carter. "Just in case Hawk's as green as he looks."

"They're already on the way."

"Excellent working with you, Chief."

"And you, Director."

Carter's image vanished.

Bowman leaned back, legs propped again, then immediately dropped them. For a moment he'd let himself think this was handled, but that twisting in his gut returned. He realized, grimly, that he'd been worrying about the wrong thing.

Catching the kids? Easy.

Dealing with what came next? That was the nightmare.

He was the Department of Magical Defense and the entire kingdom expected him to handle this monster.

He didn't even like *thinking* the creature's name.

Biriad. The karuk summoned by Alberoth. It was a brutal weapon of destruction unleashed during the Great Kingdom Wars that had proven impossible to control. Alberoth had realized too late that he had no power to command the creature, only to banish it, and only if the summoner performed a binding first.

Opal hadn't known. If only the girl had turned the page and read the next casting. If she had, she could've bound Biriad, then banished him, no matter where he ran.

Instead, Biriad was loose in a crowded world that was completely unprotected.

Bowman reached for the extra-large bottle of antacid he'd been nursing since yesterday and took a swig.

Somehow, he had to find a way to help the girl undo this. Their ancestors had forced Alberoth to banish Biriad. Surely he could convince a teenage girl to do the same.

11

JUMP!

Will followed Avo and Opal through the dimly lit service corridors, the sound of their footsteps echoing off the metal walls.

"A call came through from the Department of Magical Defense," Avo explained urgently. "They're looking for you. Best to get back in the crate."

Footsteps echoed in the hallway, and Avo stopped, looking around wildly.

"It's too late," he whispered.

He pressed his hand against a wall panel, and it slid back to reveal a janitor's closet. Avo didn't need to say anything. Will and Opal rushed inside. Tools, RoboVac parts, mops, and cleaning supplies cluttered the shelves of the tiny closet. They crammed themselves in as Avo slid the door shut. It didn't close completely, and Will could see a slice of the cargo bay through the door.

He watched as the cargo bay door burst open and guards in heavy boots stomped into the room.

"We need to see this crate." The one in front shoved a comscreen in Avo's face.

Avo slowly read it at arm's length. It was Opal and Will's crate.

"Hmmm... Yes, I think I know where that is."

He led them down several rows, pretending to search for it. Once at the crate, he opened it. The crate contained nothing but blankets and discarded water flasks. All the evidence they needed to know the kids were on the airship.

"We found the crate, but they're gone." The security guard spoke into his wristcom, then listened to the response in his earpiece. He nodded. "The lounge! Now!"

As quickly as they had come, they were gone. Avo ran to the nearest porthole, then called for Opal and Will to come out from hiding.

After they'd joined him, he said, "Quickly, you can't go back in the crate, and we can't risk getting much lower." Avo pulled two glide suits out of a wall panel.

Ever since the infamous Flint airship collision, every seat has an emergency glide suit underneath it, and every crewmember has one at their station. Avo handed one to Opal and one to Will.

"You'll have to jump. It's the only way you're getting off this airship without being caught. Hurry. You have just a few minutes."

Opal and Will fumbled with the sleek, skintight glide suits, struggling to fit them over their clothes and backpack. Avo stepped in to help, adjusting the fit and explaining the suit's features. The suits had fins that extended from the heels and calves, controlled by foot paddles; fabric flowed from ankle to wrist, creating wings; and a snug hood with a wind visor served as a padded helmet. Will's dads had taken him on his first glide just last year when they'd been on vacation up in Talosin. He lifted a foot and flexed the ankle, watching the fin react.

"How do you fly one of these?" Opal asked.

"Easy as pie," Avo said. "See the joint ribbing? It's empty tubing. We gas you up with dragozo before you jump, then you spread your arms and legs when you're in the air. The wing gives you glide; dragozo gives you buoyancy, so you won't crash. Use the rudders attached to your feet to steer. Glide west, away from the city, and keep heading west towards the treeline once you land. Eventually, you'll be in Aelliviss. Tell them you're headed for Acoena. We'll get word to them to watch for you."

Avo's eyes flicked to the porthole. "The tethers are dropping. We're losing altitude, you've got to go. Now."

Wind whistled into the bay as Avo grabbed two tubes from the wall and inserted them into each suit, filling them with dragozo.

"Jump!" Avo shouted when he was done.

Opal and Will stood locked in place, staring at the ground far below. Will's stomach twisted. They were closer to the ground than he'd expected. He glanced at Opal. Her wide eyes and locked knees said it all: she wasn't jumping unless someone made her.

"You can do this, Opal," Will said.

Opal stood in the door, staring at the ground far below, shaking her head.

There was no time to wait for her to find her courage. Avo gave them a push, and sent them flying into open air.

12

HAY THERE

Opal tumbled through the air, spinning uncontrollably, certain she was about to die. Her cheeks burned from the air rushing past.

As she had been pushed out of the airship, she saw something reddish streak towards her. Instinctively, she curled into a ball to avoid an attack. Now the world was a dizzying frenzy of colors. Which way was up? Which was down? Just as she glimpsed a flash of blue and thought she'd found the sky, it vanished. The ground spun past her in jagged blurs.

Panic took over. She screamed. Her vision darkened. Her mind was shutting down. Will's voice reached through the darkness.

"Spread your arms and legs, Opal. Fly!"

Fighting the terror, she uncurled her limbs. Her tumble stopped. She leveled out and began to glide. The dragozo in her suit slowed her fall, while the fabric wings caught the air.

Her fear retreated.

To her left, a red drago flapped away. It was probably wondering where the random, falling human had come from. Opal might have scared it more than it had scared her.

Will glided up beside her, grinning. She glanced down. There was no airship floor or window between her and the sky. She was flying. She grinned back.

West Doyova spread beneath them, not nearly as big as New Andrin, the downtown buildings were half the height. Soon, the city vanished behind them. Ahead, the flat plains rolled into forested hills and finally into the thick Aelliven forest.

Directly below were roads, fields, ponds, and grazing cattle and sheep. They passed over a farmhouse where two kids stopped playing to wave.

Will whooped, flipped onto his back, laughing. Opal tried the move and began to tumble again. This time, she quickly corrected, spread her arms, and was stable. She decided flying right side up was just fine, though she dared a few swooping turns, shouting with exhilaration.

They glided towards what they thought was the west and a distant tree line.

Then Opal realized that Avo had never explained how to land. Flying was easy, but landing might not be. Would the dragozo keep them from crashing? What if she hit a tree or a building?

Will swooped beside her again. They had drifted close enough to the ground that his aerobatics were becoming dangerous.

They passed directly over a herd of cattle. Opal mooed, wondering what they thought of the strange flying cow.

Getting closer to the ground, Opal felt like she could reach out and brush the tops of the golden grain stalks below her. She was mesmerized, until the wheat disappeared beneath her. She looked up. Time slowed as she saw a haystack directly in front of her. In an instant she was inside, flying through the prickly hay and coming to a dark and dusty stop.

Opal heard Will chuckling but then his laughter stopped. He must have landed nearby.

"Opal? Are you all right?"

She didn't answer.

"Opal?"

"Yes," her voice was muffled.

"Come out."

"I think I'll just stay in here."

"Don't be ridiculous."

He reached in and found her arm, pulling her out.

Even covered in dust and hay, she couldn't hide her red face.

"You should've left me in there. It was so nice and safe and dark."

She looked around at the rolling hills. There wasn't a house in sight.

"What do we do now?" Will asked.

"For starters, we get out of these suits," Opal said. "Then we figure out which way is west and start walking. We need to find shelter before dark."

She peeled out of her suit. "How far away do you think Aelliviss is?"

"A couple days' walk, at least," Will said, stuffing his suit in his pack.

"Why are you keeping it?"

"Seems smart. You know, 'Wasting folk are wanting folk.'"

Opal rolled her eyes but packed hers too. The sleek fabric scrunched tightly and didn't take up much space.

Will looked at the sky. "The sun's there, so that's east. That must be west."

"Maybe if we were at the equator," she said. "You're pointing north-west. Follow me."

She collected some sticks, pushed one into the dirt, and marked the shadow's tip with another. She tossed her backpack on the ground and lay down, using it as a pillow.

"Now we wait," she explained.

Will sat cross-legged in the grass beside her, twirling a blade of grass.

"I guess I can tell you now," he said.

"Tell me what?"

"My dream this morning."

She stayed quiet, so he went on.

"I saw you falling and screaming, but you weren't wearing a glide suit. I wanted to yell, but the words wouldn't come out."

He knew? He knew and didn't warn her she might be falling from an airship? It had all come out alright, but it still bothered her a little. "I should be mad," she said, "But if you had told me, I would have been freaked out the whole flight. So maybe it was better for me not to know."

"Exactly. My dreams show problems and how to fix them. This time, it was to remind you that you just had to spread your wings."

Will told her about other dreams. Opal was fascinated. She'd never met anyone who could see the future, and it actually seemed useful. Maybe her own powers weren't entirely pointless either.

"Do you think Avo will get in trouble?" Will asked.

"I doubt it. He's smart. They won't know he helped us."

"I hope you're right.

She looked at the stick's shadow next to her. It had moved.

She placed a second stick to mark the new location, drew a line between the two sticks, and pointed.

"That's west."

"How do you know?"

"Science. My mom taught me."

Opal slung her backpack over her shoulder and started walking.

Will jogged to catch up. "We make a good team," he said. "My magic, your science. We might actually survive this."

Opal didn't answer.

She wasn't quite ready to admit it, but maybe, just maybe, magic wasn't entirely useless.

13

RISE OF THE MUKDRI

F lint stood atop the crumbling tower, gazing across the rolling plains. It was a cool, crisp morning, the first he'd spent outside prison walls in decades. Sparkling dew lit the landscape, shimmering as the morning sun hit the grass. A soft breeze ruffled his hair, and made the light on the grass dance. The prairie stretched to the horizon in gentle waves, cradling the ruins of Tillers Castle.

The land and ruins had been in Flint's family for generations, though he'd grown up in a modest farmhouse nearby. Tillers Castle had once protected the farmers for forty miles in every direction. Their united strength had formed the boundaries of the Tall Grass Kingdom. The rich prairie soil produced abundant crops and provided pastureland for huge herds of cattle. The kingdom's food wealth had once made it powerful, and Flint's ancestors had ruled it all.

Farmers still used the land, but no lord or castle protected them. Community and the rule of law now kept the peace. They shared the open grasslands and came together when one of them suffered loss.

Flint saw this as a tragedy. Security had made the people soft. Without fear, they would never seek his leadership. They believed they were safe. He intended to correct that mistake.

This land was where he'd first learned fear. His father had a heavy hand, often leaving him bruised. The anger he felt after his beatings had been what opened the door to his magical ability. His fury sent objects flying.

When his father finally sent him to Aelliviss for training, Flint didn't feel gratitude. Only resentment, abandonment, and betrayal. And he meant to make others pay for his pain.

He had been a gifted student, but within a year the Aellivi sent him home.

Home. He looked at the ruins beneath his feet. Mostly piles of stone. Some sections still stood, but gaping holes scarred the walls and roof. It wasn't enough that his family's reputation had been blackened by Alberoth; the people had laid ruin to the family castle. Flint would restore it with conquest, with fear, and with fire. He would rebuild Tillers Castle.

Biriad was the perfect weapon to spread fear. But first, he had to deal with the girl who had summoned him. If done correctly, killing Opal would transfer the girl's power to control Biriad to Flint. The frightened citizens of Andrin would have no choice but to turn to him as their savior.

Flint chuckled, giddy with freedom. After decades of imagining escape, he'd never dreamed of rescue by karuk. That his family's most infamous weapon had also been his liberator, that was poetry.

He needed rest, but one more casting remained.

Flint made his way down the tower's crumbling spiral stairs, into a dark, empty chamber. Before transporting to Tillers Castle, they'd stopped by the classroom where Biriad had been summoned. From his bag, he drew out The Book of Maelogi, still marked with a smear of Instructor Miller's blood.

He skimmed the pages until he found the casting he wanted. He studied each word carefully, searching for the roots of its power. Once ready, he stood in the center of the room, the book propped open in front of him.

He had long dreamed of reading from this book. The Aellivi had kept it from him, saying it was beyond his reach. But now, here it was. And as he stared down at the inked words, fear crept in at the edges of his thoughts.

It had been a long time since he had tried to control power of this magnitude. Was he still capable? Were the Aellivi right? Would this book be beyond his abilities? Had the long years in prison dulled his gift?

His hand trembled. He began to read.

The words tumbled out in quick whispers. He had not forgotten.

His mind stretched outward. He found what he needed. Across the plains was an ancient waterhole, long known to trap the careless when rains turned its edges to mud. Centuries of bones had settled beneath its surface, beast and Drin alike, turned to fossil and stone. His voice grew stronger.

"Mukdri cranniock belsum . . ."

The room grew darker. The final words clanged against the stone walls.

". . . Akta volkum ixst."

Flint threw his head back. Energy roared through him. The room grew cold. Flint exhaled sharply; filling the air with mist.

It was done.

***

Far to the west, a herd of cattle gathered at a waterhole. It hadn't rained in weeks, yet the ground churned to thick muck beneath their hooves. Their weight broke through the crust, hooves sinking into the softened earth. Dozens of cattle pressed forward eager to soothe their thirst.

Focused on drinking, they didn't notice the mud roiling beneath them. A clawed hand burst from the muck. Several cattle bellowed, startled. A body emerged; stringy hair plastered to his mud-caked skull; eyes white, jagged stones for teeth. If it wore clothes, they were fused with the sludge. Three more emerged, smaller, leaner copies of the first.

Terror rippled through the herd. Those near the front tried to back away, but the press of cattle behind them drove them forward. Within seconds, the whole herd broke into a stampede, thundering across the prairie.

A fossilized tusk rose from the mire. The first mud-man grasped it and tugged forth a massive wild boar. Seven feet tall at its hunched shoulders. Clay dripped down its sides. It snorted, spraying silt from its nostrils.

The smaller mud men extracted their own beasts. These creatures, known as mukdri, were creatures of fossil and clay. Their bodies were armored in drying earth, and sinewed with roots and bone.

The boars pawed at the ground. The leader threw back his head and let out a bone-rattling howl. The others joined in, the boars squealing in unison.

Then silence.

The leader uttered one guttural syllable.

"Kuhk."

The mud-men swung onto their boars, kicking their flanks. The mukdri boars thundered across the prairie, ears forward, noses low. Hunting for the girl who summoned a monster.

14

MOSTLY HAY

Opal and Will walked for the rest of the day. When the sun reached its peak, they stopped to eat and check their direction. Nobody had thought to give them a map because, of course, they were never supposed to be walking across the prairie. And they'd left their wristcoms behind so they couldn't be tracked. Opal wasn't entirely sure where they were, or how far they'd glided from West Doyova. Based on hazy memories from geography class, she was pretty sure they were headed toward a major road into Aelliviss. The question was, would they hit the woods first and follow the trees to the road, or reach the road and use it to guide them into the forest?

Progress was slow. Opal stopped to inspect every flower, lizard, snake, insect, and tuft of grass along the way. Nature amazed her. She had never left New Andrin before. The city sky was a narrow strip squeezed between skyscrapers. Out here it spread in every direction. She kept asking Will questions. He answered patiently, even though he didn't know nearly enough. He couldn't name the lizard with ridges on its back, or the fuzzy flower growing in the shadows of the braiben bushes.

But thankfully, he knew about the berries. In another month or so, the deep red braiberries would have made a delicious treat. Right now they were yellow, and if eaten, they would guarantee a terrible stomachache followed by a desperate sprint to the toilet. Opal was grateful when Will stopped her from trying them. The incident opened the floodgates to a whole new round of question. Is this edible? Is that poisonous? Who figured all this out in the first place?

Eventually, Opal grew tired of hearing "I don't know," and her curiosity gave way to quiet. They plodded along in silence, her thoughts drifting. The sky no longer felt vast and beautiful - it felt huge and terrifying. They were completely exposed. If the Guard sent an aerial patrol, there'd be nowhere to hide. Every time they crested a rise, the tree line ahead seemed just as far away. It might take another full day to reach the safety of those woods.

In the late afternoon, dark clouds rolled in and a cold wind began to blow. The clouds burst, pelting them with sharp, heavy rain. With no shelter, they could do nothing but continue walking. It passed over in less than an hour, but when the sun dipped toward the horizon, they were still damp, still exposed, and hadn't found a place to camp. They surveyed the landscape from a hilltop. Will pointed out a clump of scrubby trees in a sheltered wash in the distance. The trees might even provide them wood for a fire and cover from prying eyes.

Opal trudged towards them, feeling miserable. She missed her dad. She missed her life. All her dreams were dust. She'd done something horrible. People were dead. Even if she somehow reached Aelliviss and banished the karuk, the damage was done. No matter what good she might do from here on out, she'd always be the girl who unleashed a karuk that killed people.

She thought of other places in the world she could disappear. Surubai sounded nice. She could live half-naked in the jungle, eat fruit all day, avoid people, and eventually die from some bug laying eggs under her skin. A tear slipped down her cheek. She wiped it away before Will noticed. She forced herself to focus on anything else.

It didn't take long to reach the wash. The trees were barely taller than they were, more like oversized bushes. With their glide suits draped over the tops, they created a decent shelter. They found some dry deadwood under the bushes and got a fire going to dry their damp clothes. Opal wished for something to cook, but all they had were apples and nutrition bars.

"Do you think we'll reach the woods tomorrow?" Will asked.

Opal didn't answer right away, partly because she didn't know but mostly because she was afraid she might start crying again.

"I hope so," she said at last.

"I hope we find an Aellivi soon. I remember stories about how dangerous the Aelliven forests are for Drin. When I was little, we used to rent a cabin near the border. My older brother told me that if I stepped one foot into the forest, the Aellivi would eat me and use my bones to decorate their houses."

"And you believed him?"

"I was six." Will shrugged.

"Once they know who we are, they'll have to help. They can't stop the karuk without me. They'll need us alive and healthy."

"Then I guess we'd better keep you away from haystacks."

Opal jabbed at him, but he dodged with a grin.

"You should've seen your face. Eyes wide, mouth open, and then poof! I half expected to see you pop out the other side." He added, "What was it like in there?"

"It was nice," she said. "No dumb boys laughing at me."

Seeing her crash landing through his eyes made it hard not to laugh. A smile sneaked past her defenses.

"Too bad your suit didn't have a camera. You could've made a fortune on Camera Chaos," she said.

Will picked up a stick and began to speak into it.

"Our last video came from a brilliant young man, Will Weaver," he said, mimicking the program's hostess. "And we're lucky enough to have his subject, Opal Hart, right here in our audience. Young woman, can you tell us what was going through your mind as you hit that haystack?"

"Mostly hay."

They collapsed into laughter. For a moment, everything was fine. Will had a way of pulling her out of the dark with his humor. She wouldn't have wanted anyone else with her on this adventure.

They sat beside the fire, talking about their families. Opal hoped Dr. Weaver had let her dad know she was safe. She also worried the Guard might have arrested Will's dad. She didn't say anything to Will. No point in making both of them worry.

Will eventually crawled onto their bed of leaves and grass, using his jacket as a blanket and his backpack as a pillow.

Not quite ready for sleep, Opal stepped out under the stars. Away from the firelight, the night sky opened up around her. For the first time in her life, she saw the stars without the dull haze of city lights. A million twinkling lights surrounded her. She felt dizzy. Small.

Somewhere above the horizon, she spotted the pale glow of Gotek. It was the nearest planet and based on satellite pictures, Gotek and Maead, their own planet, were similar. Maybe some kid was staring back at Maead right now, wondering if it was habitable. Maybe they'd meet one day. Maybe she'd get to see it for herself.

Remembering instructions she'd read on SkySite, she followed the trail of light from her own galaxy until she reached the nearby spiral galaxy, Sidel. Without city lights, she didn't need a spacescope. She could actually see it with her own eyes.

Contemplating life on a nearby planet was one thing. Actually seeing a whole other galaxy with billions of stars and planets, was mind-boggling. There could be billions of other kids out there, all looking up at the sky, dreaming about meeting someone like her.

Then her thoughts snapped back to Maead. She wasn't a stargazer or an explorer. She was just a scared girl, hiding in the middle of the Andrin prairie, being hunted by the Guard and a creature from another dimension.

If those billions of other kids knew what was good for them, they would stay far, far away. Her life was nothing but trouble.

15

THE PATH NOT CHOSEN

Agent Bowman resisted every urge to hurl his mug of tea across the room. It made no sense. How did this kid keep vanishing? One minute she was outside the conference room door, the next she was gone. She'd been shipped in a crate, but then the crate was empty. She was just a kid! It shouldn't be this hard.

An hour ago it had all seemed so easy. He'd done some research and learned that Alberoth had banished Biriad by first drawing him in with a casting that attracted negative energy. Biriad, unable to resist the pull, had come straight to him. Alberoth had then bound Biriad using a casting from the Book of Maellogi and banished him to another dimension.

Alberoth hadn't banished the karuk out of guilt or wanting redemption. He'd done it to save his own skin. The people of Andrin were calling for his quick and public execution. But Alberoth refused to banish Biriad unless they spared his life. They agreed, and after the banishment, they forced him to take a potion that blocked his ability to cast. He lived out his final days in a dungeon cell. Had Alberoth known he'd turn into a rambling fool in a stone box, he might have chosen differently.

Things should go easier with this girl, Bowman told himself. Opal had no training and didn't seem to need it to cast. He just needed to get the Book of Maellogi from the school.

He'd been working through that line of thought when Carter's face reappeared on his comscreen. She looked pinched and annoyed.

"They're gone," she said flatly.

"What do you mean they're gone?"

"Somehow, they escaped the airship midflight. Airship security didn't catch it until the landing. They checked the IDs of every passenger and crew member before disembarkation. A squad of my Guard swept the ship. Nothing."

Bowman slapped the desk. "Craddock take them. Where are they?"

"Our search found two emergency glide suits missing from the cargo bay. A crewmember is being questioned. We've put out alerts for any glider sightings. Judging by the elevation they jumped from; we're looking at a forty-mile radius."

"Focus to the west," Bowman said. "Everything points to the Aelliven forest. We have to stop them before they get there."

After ending the call, he sent a message to Roa. They hadn't spoken since childhood, but Roa was his only contact in the forest.

Aellivi students were sometimes allowed to attend a semester in Andrin to experience modern life. Bowman's family had hosted Roa in their home, and the two had become close. But once Roa returned home, they never spoke again.

Still, Bowman hoped that maybe, just maybe, Roa could be persuaded to help retrieve the girl quietly, without sparking a political incident.

That sliver of optimism vanished when another message came through. Pascam school security had gone to retrieve the Book of Maellogi. It was missing. Instructor Miller was dead.

Bowman pushed that new tragedy aside. His first priority was to find the girl. It was an unsettling possibility she had taken the book.

He examined the map of the West Doyova region on his comscreen. A few scattered reports placed the kids to the west. Patrols were combing the area with heat scanners. Drones were scheduled to cover the remaining sectors by midnight. So far, only livestock showed up on scans.

At least Biriad had stopped killing, for now. But Bowman had read enough to know this was no comfort. After feeding, the karuk often disappeared, then resumed killing days later. More deaths were coming.

He set his mug down with restraint and opened Opal Hart's file again, looking for something, anything, to help.

Was she seduced by power? A secret sociopath? Nothing in her records suggested that. She was a bright, moody teen. Strong in science. Destined for engineering until he redirected her path. She didn't ask for this. Maybe, he thought bitterly, he should've left her to study physics and coding instead of castings and karuks. So many lives would've been spared.

He, too, had tested high in magical ability. Unlike Opal, he wanted to become a mage. He dreamed of restoring magic to the Drin world.

And unlike Opal, Bowman came from money. His parents hadn't wanted the embarrassment of having a mage in the family. They bribed an acquaintance on the placement board, and young Gale found himself enrolled at the prestigious Mercer School of Business, studying spreadsheets while dreaming of attending the school Opal rejected. He was a good son. He obeyed, and buried his gifts.

He waved his hand and Opal's file disappeared. Leaning back, he rubbed the grit from his eyes. He'd barely slept. He closed his eyes for just a moment.

Seconds later, he slipped into the dream that had haunted him for years.

He stood on a mountain trail under a stormy sky. Lightning revealing a fork ahead. To the left: a narrow, treacherous path, dark with clouds and pouring rain. To the right: a sunny trail.

He turned toward the easier path, but with each step, the sky darkened. Rain slashed his face. The trail narrowed, shrank, and became mud. His feet slipped. He fell in an endless drop.

Then he was on the summit.

A figure stood nearby, darker than any black he'd ever seen. Around it pulsed a blinding glow, too brilliant to look at directly. It battled someone.

A small shape stood in front of it, back turned, just a silhouette against the light. For years, the figure had been unrecognizable.

But tonight, he could see clearly. Opal Hart.

Hair whipped by the wind, arms raised, she faced down the shadow.

Bowman's heart pounded. He knew what to do. He'd known for years. Bowman reached deep within himself. Power surged under his skin. He opened his mouth to cast. Nothing came out. He couldn't breathe. Couldn't speak. Couldn't help.

Energy churned inside him with nowhere to go.

He jerked upright in his seat, gasping, heart hammering.

The dream finally made sense.

The fork in the path was his career choice. He'd taken the "easy" road, but it hadn't spared him hardship. Now, he was at the summit, without the skill or power to fulfill his purpose.

But the dream had changed.

It had never shown the face of the small figure before. Now he knew it was Opal.

He had to help her.

His thoughts turned again to Roa. Years ago, Roa was the first to truly recognize Bowman's latent magic. He'd urged Bowman to study, even if only in secret. Bowman had refused to disobey his parents and they hadn't spoken since.

A plan formed.

He would go to West Doyova, not to capture Opal, but to find her. And Maybe, if Roa agreed, learn together. Fight together. Survive together.

He composed a message to Deputy Chief Tanner, saying he was heading to West Doyova to personally supervise the operation. Then he scheduled it to send a few hours later, once his flight was already underway and too far along to stop.

He booked a private airship on the department's account.

And for the first time in days, Gale Bowman smiled.

16

STALKED

Will screamed.

Opal jerked awake. "Will!" she whispered, reaching over and grabbing his shoulder.

His eyes flew open, wild and unfocused. He sucked in a choking breath, coughing hard as if something thick filled his throat. He clawed at his face, wiping away something only he could feel.

Opal shook him lightly. "It's okay. You're awake now. It's just a dream."

His eyes came into focus. Tears streamed down his cheeks, but he nodded.

She asked, "Want to tell me what it was?"

Will wiped his face with his sleeve, eyes still watery. "Mud," he said, voice hoarse. "We were in a dry riverbed. Something big came, and the whole bank just... collapsed on us. I couldn't breathe. I couldn't scream. You were beside me but not moving."

Opal frowned. "So... maybe no riverbeds for us today."

Will gave a weak laugh and nodded. "That'd be good."

As they munched on apples, Opal made a walking stick from one of the branches they'd slept under. After breakfast, they packed their things, did their best to wipe away any sign they'd camped there, and continued west toward the tree line, which still looked as distant as it had the day before.

She wondered how many more days it would take before they reached the safety of the Aelliven forest.

To the south, a few harvesting machines crept along rows of crops. They'd need to steer clear. Most were automated, but often there were people nearby to monitor and maintain them.

As the sun climbed higher, its warm glow made everything feel a little better. Even so, Will looked down. Opal came to his rescue.

"What's brown and sticky?"

Will muttered to himself. "Have I heard this one? Boogers? They are more greenish brown. Glue is usually white or clear."

He gave up. "I don't know."

"A stick!" Opal shouted, holding up the walking stick she'd made.

Will rolled his eyes. Opal tossed the stick in the air then tried to snatch it as it spun. She missed. It bounced back and smacked her in the forehead.

Will finally laughed. Opal looked at him, pretending injury.

"I'll have to remember that. Jokes? Nothing. Watching me get injured? Hysterical."

"You're fine."

They walked in silence for a while.

"You know," Will said, "sometimes I do dumb things, too. The other morning, I tried to take a picture of the fog."

"What happened?"

"Missed."

Opal didn't react. Then she got the wordplay, missed/mist, and chuckled.

"Good one."

They spent the rest of the morning, walking in silence then taking turns surprising each other with ridiculous jokes. After a few hours they took a break to eat their last apples.

"I think we'll be there by tonight," Opal said, gazing at the tree line. "Maybe we'll find some fruit trees."

"Mmm, Aelliven peaches are my favorite."

Will could almost feel the juice running down his chin, but the thought made him thirsty, so he quickly bannished it. They didn't have much water left.

They continued through fields and pastures. By early afternoon, they entered rows of tall cornstalks.

"I don't like this," Will muttered. "We won't be able to see anything."

"Nobody will be able to see us, either," Opal said. "Besides, we'll be through before you know it." She stepped into the cornfield.

Will hesitated. She turned back and waved him on.

"Come on."

He hadn't told Opal, but earlier he'd spotted black dots circling in the sky to the north. They might be crows, maybe. Or buzzards. Wild dragos, even. But he was afraid they were drones. Opal moved ahead.

"What has ears but can't hear?" she said.

"Corn!" Will shouted.

Now it was his turn. "Two ears of corn were growing in a field. One noticed that every time they swayed in the wind, something green appeared behind the other. 'Don't look now,' it said to the other ear, 'but we're being stalked.'"

Opal groaned.

By the time they emerged from the far side of the cornfield, Will had grown comfortable with the feeling of invisibility. Now, stepping into the open again, he felt exposed. He noticed Opal glance at the sky to the north.

"Have you seen them, too?" he asked.

She nodded. Apparently, they'd both been keeping secrets so the other wouldn't worry.

They did their best to keep trees, crops, bushes, or hills between them and the black dots. The terrain had grown more uneven, which helped them stay hidden, but it also slowed them down. By mid-afternoon, they had run out of water. By late afternoon, their lips were cracked and their tongues dry.

At the top of a small rise, they scanned the land. To the southwest stood a farm they'd have to avoid. A riverbed wound below them, mostly dry with scattered mud holes. One section was thick with bushes.

"Is that water?" Opal asked through cracked lips. "I think I see something sparkly."

Without a word, Will headed that direction. Opal followed.

They reached a pool of still water ringed with mud.

"It doesn't look great, but it's something," Opal said.

To get to the water, she had to step into the mud. She sank to her calves and was stuck. Will grabbed her outstretched arms and pulled her free.

"I don't think that's going to work," she said.

Opal shook a leg, trying to dislodge the mud clinging to her pants and shoes. A glob flung off and smacked Will on the nose. He crossed his eyes to stare at it. Opal laughed. Will brushed the mud from his face and started laughing, too.

Their laughter died instantly at the sound of galloping. They dove into the bushes.

The creatures were closing in. He remembered the first part of the dream when something had been chasing them. The rhythm matched. There were four rapid steps followed by a pause, and not the sharp clatter of hooves, but a wet, smacking gallop.

Harsh guttural voices speaking a strange language filtered through the leaves directly above them. Opal and Will held their breath. Will craned his neck and glimpsed mud-caked men with glittering white eyes.

A voice called out nearby. The creatures moved several hundred yards away. At their new location, Will and Opal could see them more clearly, men coated in mud, some walking beside massive, mud-covered boars, others riding them. Mud dripped from their bodies endlessly. Will recognized them from childhood stories.

"They're mukdri," he whispered. "And they're hunting us. My dream... We have to go."

"But they'll see us."

"If we stay, they'll find us."

He pointed to a spot up the riverbank, shielded by brush. They moved quietly, and Opal grabbed roots to pull herself up, thorns snagging her clothes. Once up, she turned and helped Will. They crouched beneath low branches.

"Let's try for the farmhouse," Will said. It was a gamble. The people there might save them from the mukdri only to turn them in to the Guard. But it was better than staying.

They crouched low, running as fast as that position allowed. For a moment, Will believed they might escape unseen.

A shout came from behind them. Will glanced over his shoulder. Four mukdri boars and riders thundered toward them. He pictured the boars' tusks catching him mid-stride.

"Run!" he screamed.

They bolted, legs pumping, lungs heaving.

They raced through a gully into a wide floodplain scattered with driftwood and pebbles. No cover. Just open space and the sound of hooves.

They scrambled up a low hill. Above, a security drone buzzed against the sky.

Will chanced a glance back. The mukdri were gaining on them. Panic surged, and he pulled ahead, grabbing Opal's hand and yanking her forward. At the top of the hill, he spotted a cockleberry orchard - rows of trees like oversized cockleburs. The gap between rows was just wide enough for a harvester, or two desperate kids.

They dove into the branches, the thorny trees slashing at their arms and faces. Behind them, the leader howled.

At first, the trees didn't slow the creatures down. But then the sharp branches began gouging deep into the mukdri, tearing away mud and bone alike. Within seconds, nothing was left but clumps of mud and scattered bones.

Will skidded to a halt, breathing hard. Opal charged ahead until he called out, "Opal! They're gone."

She stopped. They both listened.

Silence.

"They couldn't get through the trees," Opal said.

"There might be some left who didn't go in."

"Let's take a chance on the farm. If we move fast, maybe we'll beat them there."

They moved slower through the thorns.

"Got any cockleberry tree jokes?" Opal said.

"Nope." Now was not the time for jokes.

They emerged onto a dirt lane, flanked by tall hedges and fields. In the distance, grain towers rose beyond the hills.

"Do you think they'll turn us in?" Opal asked.

"We've got a better chance with a farmer than mukdri or drones. People out here don't trust the government much."

Turning a corner, they froze. Opal's arm shot out, shielding Will. A man stood in the road, pointing a sonic rifle at them. He wore tight leggings, a simple tunic, and a bag slung across his chest. Gray hair blew wildly around his bearded face.

"Don't shoot!" Opal called out. "We're not stealing or anything."

"But you are trespassing. What are you doing on my land?"

"We were trying to get away from..." Will began.

"Those drones harassing my cattle?"

"Yes," said Will, just as Opal answered, "No!"

The man narrowed his eyes. "Well, which is it?"

Will and Opal exchanged a look. Finally, Opal answered.

"First we ran from the mukdri. Then the drones."

"Mukdri? They haven't been seen in centuries," the man said. "You sure that's what they were?"

"They were men made of mud riding giant wild boars made of mud," Opal said. "So, yeah."

"Why are they chasing you? How did you lose them?"

"We lost them in your cockleberry orchard," Will said.

"They came in after you?"

"They did. At least some of them did."

"Then we might have some time. Come with me."

They followed him. What choice did they have? If someone was offering help, they had to take the chance.

***

Back in the orchard, clumps of mud slipped from branches, slapping wetly onto the ground. Slowly, they oozed together, dragging toward the bones. The hunt wasn't over. The mukdri would rise again.

17

NOTHING TO SEE HERE

Bowman stepped off the private airship and looked around to get his bearings. The land stretched flat in all directions, except to the north where jagged peaks rose in dramatic contrast above the prairie. The air was brisk, cooler than in New Andrin, without a cloud in the sky, a perfect afternoon for a manhunt... or a kidhunt, in this case.

Chief Carter approached in a crisp Guard uniform, offering a wide, open smile. Luckily for Bowman, she knew nothing of his impending firing. She updated him on their progress as they walked toward the rover the local Guard had assigned him. It was a beast of a machine, an off-road vehicle set on six independent wheels that could adapt to nearly any terrain. In rougher landscapes, treads deployed over the wheels to make it nearly unstoppable. The cab seated four and was encased in a steel frame topped with a flexiglass dome for a full 360-degree view.

"Nothing. We've seen nothing," Carter said as she slid into the rover. "Well, we've seen one thing, but it turned out to be nothing."

Bowman took the seat to her right. He pulled the control console toward him.

"You're telling me there's been no sign of them? Nobody's found the glide suits? Anything?"

"That's correct, sir. We based our search pattern on eyewitness accounts who saw them fly over. No one has spotted them on the ground."

"You mentioned something was seen, but it turned out to be nothing?"

"One of our drone pilots thought he saw two people being chased by riders on horseback. But when he repositioned for a better look, they were gone. There was a large cockleberry orchard nearby. If it was the kids, they may have hidden there. But the horses would've had nowhere to go. We think it was a digital glitch of some sort."

Bowman pulled out his comscreen. With a few taps, he brought up the search grid.

"Which sector?" he asked.

Carter pointed to sector K3.

"How long would it take to get there?"

"An hour or so. But why bother? It was nothing."

"You're probably right. No need to waste your time, but I'd like to see for myself."

"Sorry. You go, I go. Policy requires me to stay with the vehicle," she said, leaving no room for discussion.

Bowman started the motor. The rover pulled away silently. At first, he'd admired Carter's competence, but now, he worried she might be too competent.

Carter pulled the controls to her side, programmed their route, and then let auto-drive handle the rest. Within minutes, they were speeding eastward down the causeway.

"How long have you been with the Department of Magical Defense?" Carter asked.

"Fifteen years," Bowman answered curtly. With all the laws he was about to break, the last thing he needed was a budding friendship. She'd thank him for his rudeness later. "Could you send me the search reports? I'd like to go over them. Is there footage from the drone?"

She tapped her comscreen. The reports appeared on his device.

He scrolled through them. As expected, nothing useful. Still, he needed to think, and scanning the files gave him cover to do so in silence.

The two running figures were glitchy, indistinct, but the galloping forms were clearer. As the drone moved in, the view cut off behind the orchard's canopy.

It was impossible to say if it was real or a malfunction, but Bowman's gut said it was real. The map showed a farmhouse near the orchard, which would be the most likely place they would go. He'd head there.

But first, he had to lose Carter.

He weighed his options. Forcing her out of the rover at gunpoint would only increase the speed at which they discovered he was no longer following orders. The best course was to send her off on some crazy mission. For that to succeed, she had to trust him. If he remained cold and withdrawn, that would be harder to pull off.

He turned off his comscreen.

"I'm sorry," he said. "I didn't mean to be rude. I'm just... distracted. My job's on the line."

He offered her a smile.

"I understand."

"How long have you been with the Guard?" he asked.

"My dad was a Guardsman. When I was just eleven . . ."

Carter's voice faded into the background. Bowman nodded and smiled as she spoke, but his mind was elsewhere, turning over excuses, looking for just the right errand that might get Carter out of the way long enough to find Opal.

18

NIGHTFALL

Opal felt a surge of energy as the sun dropped behind the nearby tree line. If she and Will left tomorrow morning, they'd reach Aelliviss before noon. All they had to do was convince the farmer to help them. Will and the farmer trudged along the path in silence. When Opal tried to ask a question, the farmer shushed her and stared at the sky, scanning for drones.

The road took a sharp turn. Opal imagined an old stone farmhouse tucked among the grain towers, maybe with a pen of cattle or sheep and the warm scent of supper drifting from the kitchen. She pictured the farmer's wife pulling a roast from the oven. She and Will hadn't had a hot meal since breakfast on the airship and had been surviving on apples and nutrition bars ever since.

Her hopes collapsed when they reached the property. There were no barns, no animals, no cozy houses. Just grain towers. Each tower rose from a base of weathered stone, probably dating back to the Kingdom Wars, with newer steel additions rising above them, doubling their height and capacity.

The farmer continued plodding toward the only tower without a steel extension. He opened a door and Opal half expected grain to pour out. Instead, it opened into a cluttered entryway. Coats hung on hooks. A rug, crusted with dried mud, sat beside a raised grate covered in scraped-off dirt. A pile of dirty overalls lay next to an empty gun rack.

The farmer closed the door, slid the deadbolt into place, and dropped two thick metal bars into wall-mounted brackets. The crossbars looked impossible to break.

"Leave your shoes there," the farmer said, pointing to the rug. "Don't want you tracking dirt up."

He slipped off his boots and climbed the stairs in his socks, still carrying the rifle. Opal and Will followed. On the next floor, the farmer flipped a switch, revealing a messy but fairly modern room, cluttered and dusty. A vidscreen hung on the wall, and a logicomp sat on a desk.

"May we have some water?" Opal asked. She had never been so thirsty.

"Yes, please," Will added, "We haven't had much to drink today."

The farmer poured them each a tall glass of water from the faucet.

They drained their glasses greedily.

He gestured toward the sink. "Help yourself to more if you want."

They filled the glasses again, and guzzled those, too. Then they sipped more slowly from the third.

"Sit," he said, motioning to the couch.

Opal and Will shifted some books and magazines, and sat, clutching their glasses.

The farmer walked to each narrow window, peered out, and then pulled the heavy curtains closed. After bolting a hatch over the stairwell, he sat down at his logicomp and tapped the sensepad. SECURITY SYSTEM ENGAGED. He spun his chair to face them, arms crossed.

"So," he said giving them a long look, "what are two city kids doing this far out in the country? And why are mukdri chasing you?"

"Who says we're city kids?" Opal snapped.

They were, of course, but the label irked her.

"Your clothes, your shoes, and your accent. New Andrin, I'd guess."

"We were traveling to Aelliviss and got separated from our guide," Will said. "We thought if we kept heading west, we'd hit the woods and follow them to the Acoena highway."

"You're pretty far off track," the farmer said. "You're two days walk south of the highway. That still doesn't explain the mukdri or the drones. Who are you?"

Opal and Will exchanged a look, unsure how much to reveal. Finally, Opal decided to tell part of the truth.

"We're nobody special. We're students at Pascam School of Magic in New Andrin. His dad arranged for us to go to Aelliviss for a while. I don't really understand why those things were after us."

"Maybe you were just convenient prey," the farmer said. "Let's hope they stop chasing you. Just in case, we need to prepare."

Opal couldn't help herself, questions tumbled out. "How do you fight mukdri? What preparations do we need to make? And what do we call you?"

The farmer chuckled. "Aren't I a fine fool. Haven't even told you my name. I'm Louir Mason. Yours?"

"I'm Opal Hart."

"Will Weaver."

"It's nice to meet you, Opal Hart and Will Weaver."

"Louir," Will said, "isn't that an Aelliven name?"

"It is. My grandmother was Aellivi."

Opal pressed forward. "Do you live out here alone? Can you help us get to Acoena?

"I do live alone. And yes, I can help get you there. As for fighting the mukdri, I've already turned on the outer security system. If anything moves, we'll know. But we've got more prep to do on the roof."

Louir crossed the room to a darkened corner, where a steel ladder was bolted to the stone wall, leading to a trap door.

The kids followed him up the ladder to the roof.

A low wall about three feet high rimmed the circular tower. Opal peered over the edge, then quickly backed away. A fall from that height might not kill her, but it would definitely hurt.

Louir opened a metal box in the center of the roof, and lifted out a coiled hose. "Hold this," he said, handing the nozzle to Will. Then he dragged the other end to a nearby valve, attaching it, and flipped a lever. "Hold tight," Louir warned. The hose writhed as it filled with water.

Opal jumped in to help, gripping the hose as it twisted in their hands. Together, they managed to wrangle it until Louir returned with a tripod. He set it up, then attached the nozzle to the mount, relieving them of their struggle.

"High-powered water cannon," he explained. "Useful for putting out prairie fires that burn too close to the towers, taking down drones, or driving off predators and unwanted guests. Tonight that means your mukdri."

Opal's eyes lit up. "Can I try?"

Louir nodded and motioned her over. "See that big can down there? I burn my trash in it. Aim for that, then pull the lever."

Opal followed his instructions. A heavy jet of water blasted out, falling short of the can. She tilted the hose up, firing again and sent the can tumbling across the yard. She grinned at Louir. This was fun.

Next Louir hauled a large case from the bottom of the metal box, set it in the center of the roof, and opened the lid. Inside, neat rows of sonic grenades glinted beside more lethal explosives.

"I'm guessing you've never used these," he said. "If the mukdri show up, use the sonic grenades. Pull the tab, press this button on the bottom, and throw within five seconds. If the hose and the sonics don't work, I, and only I, will throw the explosives. Clear?"

Opal nodded, relieved. She loved things that went boom but was glad to leave the serious firepower to Louir.

With preparations complete, they climbed down the ladder. Louir started putting together supper while Will and Opal hovered nearby, unsure how to help. He opened the refrigerator, which matched the rest of the place: cluttered, crowded, and more than a little dirty. Some of the glass containers inside were filled with green, slimy substances that made Opal want to gag.

"Does the vidscreen work?" she asked, desperate for a distraction.

"I guess. Haven't turned it on in months. Glove should be by the chair."

Opal and Will collapsed into two overstuffed chairs facing the vidscreen. Opal wondered why Louir had two chairs when he lived alone, and why he had no spouse or kids.

The control mechanism was more a harness than a glove. It tightened automatically to fit her hand. She waved, and the screen flared to life; bright, loud, and chaotic. She quickly wiggled her fingers to lower the volume.

Flicking through the channels brought a relentless stream of game shows and overwrought dramas. Finally, she landed on a news channel. She wanted to know what was happening back home, and what was happening with the karuk.

After a string of commercials, the newsreader, a slender woman with long, sleek hair, reappeared.

"Our top story: it has been two days without any reported deaths or sightings of the karuk that tore through New Andrin. At last count, thirty-four people died in the attack."

Opal's stomach turned. She wished she'd never been born.

"The Guard continues to search, not only for the karuk," the newsreader went on, "but for two children believed to be involved. If you see either of them, please contact the Guard immediately."

Opal and Will's pictures filled the screen. She winced. They'd used last year's school photo. She looked like such a baby. Will looked so serious. Nothing like the funny kid she'd come to know.

Opal quickly flipped her hand. The channel changed to the weather. She glanced behind her. Louir was still at the stove, seemingly focused on the meal. Hopefully, he hadn't been paying attention.

Despite the refrigerator's grim contents, the food smelled amazing.

The food had barely hit the table before the kids dove in, piling their plates high and eating so fast they barely chewed.

Then Louir broke the silence.

"That lady on the news," he said. "Was she right? Did you have something to do with the karuk that killed all those people?"

Will found his voice first.

"We didn't mean to. It was an accident. Now they want to lock up Opal to study her. We're trying to reach the Aellivi. We think they can help stop that thing."

"That explains the drone and the mukdri," Louir said.

As if on cue, an eerie, wet howl rose outside. The perimeter alarms beeped.

Opal's stomach lurched. She felt like she might throw up.

Louir calmly put down his knife and fork. "To the roof. Now."

They scrambled up the ladder. Opal leaned over the roof and saw mukdri galloping into the yard. Security lights flared on, illuminating the scene. For the first time, she got a close look at them. They were moving clay sculptures with glinting stone tusks and empty eyes. They were a nightmare come to life.

"Where do they come from?" she asked.

"Below," Louir replied, his voice steady. "They are magic, mud, and bones. I need you to spot. I've got the hose. Grab those sonics and use them when they get close. Let's hope the blast is strong enough to shatter the mud."

Will and Opal filled their jacket pockets with round black grenades. They patrolled the tower walls. The building wasn't that tall. With coordination, the mukdri could get onto the roof easily. So far, they weren't trying. She watched the boars circle, snorting as their riders looked up, mouths gaping, exposing sharp, uneven teeth.

Louir placed the tripod and opened fired. The high-pressure stream slammed into the mukdri. Will tossed a grenade. A moment later, it exploded with a concussive whump, scattering mud and splintered bone. One boar and rider collapsed into sludge and shards. Louir kept spraying, pushing the remains farther from the tower.

A squelch behind her made Opal whip around. A mukdri was climbing on the shoulders of another. "Over here!" she shouted as she dropped a grenade.

Louir rushed to her and washed the mukdri away in a stream of mud.

Opal watched in horror. The muck was moving. Bones were snapping into place. A clawed hand twitched, as it reached for the empty sockets of its skull. The mukdri were reforming.

"They're back!" she shouted. "We can't stop them. They just come back."

Louir's face was grim. He opened the valve, blasting a climbing mukdri. Behind them, Will and Opal threw grenades one after another, their percussive blasts splitting mud men and boars apart, but not for long.

"This isn't working!" Will yelled.

"Take the hose," Louir said, thrusting the nozzle at Opal. "Keep spraying."

He reached into the case and pulled out the explosive grenades.

"Headlights coming!" Will's voice cracked with fear.

Opal turned. Through the hedgerows, beams of flickering light cut across the field as a vehicle approached.

Louir picked his target and threw.

The grenade detonated behind two mukdri climbing up the wall, causing boars and riders to disintegrate into dust. No bones remained for the mud to cling to.

The rest of them scattered into the darkness.

Silence fell.

The car, now at the house, flooded the yard with light. A door opened, but the driver remained hidden behind the glare of the headlights.

"Hello?" a voice called out. "Agent Gale Bowman, Department of Magical Defense. I'd like to have a word with you."

Opal's stomach sank. One danger had passed, but another had just arrived.

19

UNLIKELY ALLIES

Bowman had spent a frustrating couple of hours, meeting with search teams and department heads. He finally escaped when they stopped at a diner, casually driving off while Carter was in the bathroom. She'd be furious, but there was a world to save.

As he prepared to turn off his comscreen, a mysterious message came through, routed through West Doyova.

"Got your message. Watching. We'll connect. Roa."

Bowman didn't know exactly what Roa meant. He'd worry about it later, after he found Opal.

He locked in the rover's navigation maps and disconnected it from the InfoMax so no one could track him. He sped down unfamiliar dirt roads, thankful they were so sparsely traveled. It was dark by the time he finally neared the remote farm.

A burst of light illuminated trees, grain towers, and clouds of smoke. There were several explosions. Bowman worried he was too late.

As he turned the final corner. Giant prehistoric mud-covered boars and men surrounded the lowest tower. On the roof, several people fought them off. A massive explosion disintegrated two of the creatures. The rest fled. Bowman waited in the rover to make sure they weren't coming back, then stepped out and called toward the tower.

"Hello? Agent Gale Bowman, Department of Magical Defense. I'd like to have a word with you."

A pause.

"What about?" a man's voice answered.

"A couple of kids are missing and in danger. Possibly being chased by the things that attacked you. I'm trying to find them. Have you seen them?"

A rusty creak echoed from above. A heavy door slammed. Silence.

Then, the security lights flicked off. Bowman felt vulnerable in the darkness.

A door swung open at the bottom of the tower. A warm beam of light spilled out, hiding the man's face.

"I'm Louir Mason," the voice said. "Thanks for helping scare off the mukdri. Come in."

Inside, Bowman assessed the farmer: lanky and graying, with a shaggy beard and flyaway hair. Crow's feet bracketed his eyes. Probably late middle age. Likely a bachelor, or a widower.

"Take off your shoes," Louir said. "Don't like to track dirt in."

Bowman complied, noticing two pairs of kid-sized shoes already on the mat.

In the cluttered house, he noted three half-eaten meals on the table. Bowman followed Louir to the sitting area, where he sank into a plush chair. Louir sat across from him, almost swallowed by a sagging sofa.

After a moment, Bowman decided to go with the truth.

"Those creatures weren't the only thing I've had to deal with lately," he said. "I don't know if you've seen the news from the capital."

"Saw a bit of it tonight," Louir responded.

"I think the mukdri might be related to the karuk terrorizing New Andrin. Magical beasts like that haven't roamed Andrin in thousands of years. The children I'm looking for are involved. I need to find them. If I don't, things will get worse."

"I wish you every success," Louir replied. "But I'm not sure what you want from me."

"You're here alone?"

"I am."

"No wife?"

"She found life on the farm boring and left for the city."

"No kids?"

"No."

"Then why are there three plates on your table?"

Louir squirmed, then answered, "Some neighbors were over."

"There were two pairs of kid's shoes in your entryway. And who was on the roof with you?"

Louir faltered. For a moment, the mask slipped. Then he recovered.

"They left before you came in. I told them not to go, but I'm not their father. They were free to do as they wished."

"They left without shoes?"

"Maybe they had other shoes in their packs."

"You think you're protecting them," Bowman said, voice tightening. "But you're not. I'm here against orders because I believe that if the government gets Opal, it'll be a disaster. She needs to get to the Aellivi. No one in Andrin can teach her what she needs to know. If the Guard finds them first, there'll be no end to the suffering. Are they on the roof?"

"They are not. Go see for yourself."

Bowman climbed the ladder and pulled himself into the cool night air. The roof was empty.

Louir joined him. "There's nothing up here but the water cannon."

Bowman spotted the metal box. Two kids could fit inside, but it was empty too. No stairs, no ladder. He frowned.

Returning to the main room, he blinked in disbelief. Standing before him were Opal and Will. All his fears and all his hopes were right in front of him.

"What are you doing?" Louir asked as he climbed down the ladder.

"We believe him," Opal said. "We want him to take us to Aelliviss."

"But after we finish eating," added Will.

As the food was reheated, Bowman watched the kids clear off a spot at the table for him. Playful and teasing, they weren't criminal masterminds or escape artists. They really were just normal kids.

Bowman thought he knew the answer, but he had to ask anyway. "Do you have the Book of Maellogi?"

They both shook their heads.

"The last time I saw it was in the classroom," Opal answered.

Just as he'd suspected, they had nothing to do with the missing book. That meant it was probably in Flint's hands. He hoped the Aellivi knew the castings Opal would need. Louir interrupted his thoughts.

"Who do you know in Aelliviss?"

"His name is Roa."

"Roa from Allos?" Louir grinned. "He's my cousin. Before you showed up, I was planning to take them to him."

Louir dug through a pile of papers on his desk and brought one to the table with him. He pushed a tattered map toward Bowman.

"Take this map of Aellivi's trail network. If you enter the forest near here, you'll hit this path. Follow it to this overnight. I'll send word to Roa."

"What's an overnight?" Will asked.

"Shelters scattered throughout the forest: lean-tos and cabins, stocked with supplies," Louir answered.

"Can you get a message to my dad? Tell him I'm okay?" Opal asked.

"I'll be sure he knows."

She turned to Bowman, "Have you talked to him? Is he okay?"

"Your dad is worried but fine."

"He hasn't been arrested or anything?"

"He has not."

"Truth?"

"Truth."

She relaxed.

"What about my dad?" Will asked.

Bowman hesitated.

"He's been detained for helping you. He'll face charges, but I doubt they'll stick, especially if you and the Aellivi stop Biriad. He can argue he acted in the kingdom's best interest."

Will blinked hard, his face pinched with worry.

"Do you think the Aellivi will help?" Opal asked.

Bowman was about to answer when the perimeter alarms blared.

Louir looked out a window.

"There are cars coming up the lane," he said. "Several cars."

Bowman hadn't thought Carter would figure it out this quickly.

He had to get the kids off this farm.

Now.

20

INTO THE WOODS

Opal had seen AT rovers on vidscreens but never in person. They were even cooler than she'd imagined. She watched Bowman press a series of buttons. The cab rose, and with a number of precise adjustments, a set of treads deployed over the tires. They needed to leave the roads behind if they wanted to avoid being captured.

Louir came running from the house, shouting.

"Go! Go! They're almost here."

He tossed a sack into the rover. Opal and Will piled into the front seat beside Bowman, who leaned out the window.

"Thanks for your trust, Louir. I'm sorry for whatever trouble this brings you. When I'm able, I'll try to help."

"I'm guessing you'll be pretty busy sorting out your own problems with the kingdom," Louir replied. "Don't worry. I'll be fine."

Bowman sped out of the farmyard, heading into the hills.

They drove fast across a dark pasture.

"I can't see anything," Opal said. "Aren't you worried you'll hit something?"

Bowman tapped a screen on the console. "Nightview," he explained. "Your eyes will adjust soon, but for now, just trust this."

The screen showed the landscape she couldn't see with her eyes, including cattle blinking in surprise as the rover disturbed their sleep.

A burst of light behind them lit up the inside of the cab. Opal and Will turned to see the farm's security lights blazing and Guard rovers swarming the yard. Tiny figures scurried about. Opal hoped Louir would be all right. It seemed like no matter what she did, she got people in trouble.

"Do you think they saw us leave?" Will asked.

"I'm sure they didn't," Bowman said, "or they'd already be following us."

"Then we're safe?"

"I didn't say that."

Will grabbed the sack Louir had thrown into the car.

"What did he give us?" Opal asked.

"A loaf of bread, flasks of water, and I think some apples."

He dropped the sack on the floor. It clanked. He reached inside.

"Oops. Those aren't apples. They're grenades."

Bowman grinned.

Opal's eyes were starting to adjust. The cattle were now behind them. The rover dodged clumps of trees as they moved through the rolling hills. They drove in silence, the kids keeping watch behind them. From each hilltop, they glimpsed Louir's farm through scattered trees. After a few minutes without being followed, Opal began to relax. The tree line loomed ahead. They were going to make it.

Then the rover rocked violently. Opal flew across the seat and slammed into Will.

Another jolt.

They were being rammed.

Bowman worked the control panel furiously. "I can't see," he muttered.

A familiar wet howl rose behind them. The mukdri were back. Cold dread flooded Opal.

Bowman's fingers flew across the console, engaging the auto-drive. Another jolt sent grenades rolling onto the floor. Will scrambled after them.

"Can you see the mukdri, Opal?" Bowman shouted.

"It's too dark. Aren't they on the nightview?"

"They don't give off heat. I'll have to risk the lights."

"The Guard will see us."

"I can't blow up what I can't see."

He switched on the headlights. A mukdri appeared instantly, tusks gleaming as the rider reached for the car. The rover was rocked again. Bowman's head smacked the window.

The rover steadied, moving forward on auto-control. Bowman sat dazed.

"Agent Bowman?" Will asked. "Are you okay?"

Bowman turned to Will, his eyes vacant. "Ahm fuhn . . ."

"He's not fine," Opal said. "Give me the grenades."

"What are you going to do? You'll blow us up."

"We have to do this."

She grabbed the grenades.

Her physics and geometry lessons came into play. As a mukdri neared her side, Opal calculated distance, arc, and trajectory. She slid down the window, pulled the tab, pressed the button, and tossed. The mukdri evaporated in a cloud of dust.

Opal cheered until another mukdri began to close in. The autopilot was taking them up a steep slope and if the beast hit them, the rover would roll.

She opened the window and tossed another grenade without any calculations.

It exploded too close to them and the force of the blast sent the rover tumbling. Opal felt herself being tossed against Will, then the ceiling, then the door, then Will again. Cries of pain and shattering glass sounded all around her. Then silence. The ATV landed upside down.

Opal groaned, tangled up with Will. Bowman dangled above them, still clipped in with his seat belt.

The second impact seemed to have cleared his head. "Get out so I can drop. Quickly."

Opal crawled through shattered glass, squeezing out. She helped Will out next. He had a cut on the bridge of his nose but otherwise looked okay. Bowman thudded onto his shoulders, crawled free, then returned to grab the sack.

"No grenades left," he said. "We have to get to the forest."

They ran, stumbling and tripping over grass and vines. The dark band of forest teased them with safety. Headlights flared, silhouetting the galloping mukdri.

Opal sprinted up the hill, passing Will and the huffing Bowman.

They burst into the dark woods. The mukdri, not far behind, skidded to a stop just outside the tree line. Opal, Will, and Bowman stopped running to look back as they gasped for air.

A mud man howled. But they didn't follow.

They looked at each other, smiles creeping onto their faces. They were safe! Will began to laugh.

Bright lights pierced the forest.

"Are you in there, Bowman?" came Carter's voice. "You need to bring that girl in."

They watched from the protection of the trees, their smiles gone, but Carter didn't come after them. Treaties forbade it. Fear enforced it.

Bowman motioned them to move deeper into the forest.

Opal's breath had slowed, and she began to look around. Opal had imagined the Aelliven forest to be a magical place where plants glowed in the dark and pixie flies danced playfully around your head. This was just a regular dark forest. Her eyes adjusted enough to see shapes but not enough to move quietly. They thrashed through branches like clumsy grommels in a percussion store.

A branch whipped Opal's cheek.

"Ow!"

"Shhh," Will said.

"I think the forest already knows we're here," she muttered. "This is how it kills us. Death by a thousand branch slaps."

"We are safe here," Bowman assured them.

"Why?" Opal asked. "We're not Aellivi."

"They know we are here, so the forest won't harm us.

Bowman stopped in a clearing and used his e-torch to light up the map.

"We need to head left. There's a path to an overnight."

For the first time, Opal had no questions. The long hike, days of fear, and adrenaline draining from her body after their escape left her too tired to care about anything. Bowman could lead her off a cliff right now and she'd gladly follow if it meant she could rest. Opal stumbled. Will grabbed her hand, squeezing it.

"Just a little farther."

Eventually, they found a wide path. It led to a stream, where a lean-to shelter and fire pit waited.

Bowman built a fire, then made beds for them.

Will croaked, "Is there any water?"

Bowman pulled some bags of water out of the shelter and handed them to the kids. Opal, half-asleep, kept trying to thank him, but her thoughts drifted away before she could speak.

He helped Will to a mat and tucked his jacket over him.

"Good night, Will. Sleep deep. I'll keep watch."

Opal stumbled into the shelter. She wrapped her arms around Bowman in a sudden hug. He held her tightly.

"Thank you," she whispered.

"You're welcome, Opal."

"Can you get us to Acoena?"

"We'll keep following the map until we get there or Roa finds us."

For the first time in days, Opal felt truly safe.

She was asleep within seconds.

21

CRICKETS AND BLOOD

In the dungeon of crumbling Tillers Castle, Flint crouched on all fours and slammed his fist into the ground. His thoughts searched for the slim threads of life he'd given the mukdri. He didn't hear their howls of defeat with his ears, but he heard them nonetheless. The girl was lost to him. He uttered a string of soft words. The thread snapped, and their muddy lives snuffed out. The mukdri vanished into the earth from which they had risen.

His frustration exploded into a scream.

The karuk was wasting time, hunting in remote rural areas. Flint needed Biriad to fill entire communities with fear. Only then would the people flock to him. Only then could he swoop in and save them.

He climbed the winding stairs to the surface, emerging into a ruined room with only three walls and an encroaching tree. He couldn't run a kingdom from here. He longed for his ancestor's stronghold to the north. Because it was deep in Dragon territory, no one knew if Varsik Castle still stood or if the retreating dragon army had razed it two thousand years ago. If it was intact, perhaps Alberoth had left behind something valuable: casting books, journals, instructions. Treasures beyond price, moldering in some forgotten vault.

But because he'd never been there, Flint couldn't transport directly. It was like knowing a site existed on the InfoMax without the address. The closest he'd ever been was the remote village of Loevashn where Flint and his father had visited an ailing aunt as a child. Life on the northern border was hard, and his aunt's weakness burdened her neighbors.

He'd watched in horror as his father smothered his own sister in her bed. Afterward, his father had explained it was her wish. It was tradition. She had become a burden, and it was his duty to end her suffering.

At the time, Flint marveled at her strength and sacrifice. Years later, he learned there was no such tradition. His father had been obligated to compensate those who'd cared for her and killed her to avoid paying.

By then, Flint had decided it didn't matter. She wouldn't have recovered. She should have been grateful. His father had freed her.

Flint shook off the memory. It wouldn't help him conquer Andrin.

He needed to go north.

He would have preferred to leave Biriad behind and let him sow terror, but the journey could be dangerous, and he could use a bodyguard. Better to convince the creature to come along.

He wondered when Biriad would return. It could be hours. Or days.

Claws scraped across cobblestones.

Was it Biriad? Or something worse?

"Biriad?" he called softly.

The hulking shadow filled the archway.

Flint's heart hammered in his chest. Whenever he was near the creature, he had to breathe deeply to calm the fear that rose.

Biriad had a large, bloody sack slung over one shoulder. He dumped it on the floor. A flatland deer carcass spilled out.

"I brought you supper," the karuk's voice rumbled.

Flint had to admit it was thoughtful. Perhaps Biriad felt some camaraderie with him after all. He could use that to his advantage.

"Thank you. We need to head north to Alberoth's castle. We can't command an army from this ruin."

"What about the girl?"

"She is beyond our reach for now."

"And how many years has it been since a Drin was at Varsik Castle? Is it even standing?"

"I don't know."

"And if it is nothing but a pile of rocks?"

"We make another plan. And if that fails, we make another one. And another."

Power surged through Flint, fueled by his fury and purpose. He had the same cold strength his father had shown in Loevashn, but even more, he had vision.

"I will not fail, Biriad. Do you understand? I have learned from Alberoth's mistakes. But I need you. I need you to do what I ask."

Biriad's eyes narrowed.

Flint held his gaze. He could feel the karuk measuring him, deciding whether to follow him or feed on him. Flint knew how important this moment was. If he showed any weakness, Biriad would devour him. Time slowed. Sweat beaded along his scalp. He would not look away from the smoldering eyes.

At last, Biriad nodded.

Elation surged through Flint. He had won.

"I can transport us as far as Loevashn. After that, we're on foot."

"Let's go," said Biriad, lifting the deer carcass again.

Moments later, nothing but the crickets remained, along with the scent of blood, slowly cooling on ancient stone.

22

THE RIVER TO ACOENA

Will and Opal sat in a boat, laughing, floating on a glassy stream. Will couldn't remember why they were laughing, but it felt so good it didn't matter. The sun's warmth pulled him towards sleep until a shadow passed overhead. He and Opal looked up, hands shading their eyes from the bright sunlight. A dragon dove straight at them, jaws wide, spouting fire.

Will awoke and lay still, eyes closed, trying to clear his head. His memories were a jumble, tangled up with his dream. Where was he this morning? He opened his eyes.

He had to be dreaming. A dragon perched on a nearby rock stared back at him.

Okay, not a dragon. A drago. In fact, it looked a lot like that red drago they'd seen in the alley. It continued watching him, it's glittering black eyes rarely blinking.

Will looked around and remembered he was in the Aelliven forest with Opal and Agent Bowman. He blinked. The drago blinked back.

"Hello," he said quietly.

Being deep in the magic of the Aelliven forest, Will half expected it to answer. It didn't. It just stared.

Opal still dozed on her mat, mouth open, breathing deeply. Bowman was nowhere to be seen.

Will turned back to the drago and whispered, "Can I help you?"

It turned, unfurled its leathery wings and flew off.

Will crawled out of the lean-to, stretching the stiffness from his arms and legs. The fire had burned to embers. He tossed on a few twigs, blew gently, and watched as small flames began to lick at the wood. He held his hands over the flames, soaking in its warmth.

A soft, chittering noise made him look up. The drago dropped a fish, which landed neatly at his feet.

"Thank you," Will said. "That's very kind of you. A hot breakfast will be delicious, even if it's fish."

Whether the drago understood him or not, it glided away.

Will set to work. He built up the fire then turned to the fish. He and his dads used to fish a lot, so he knew what to do, even if he'd only ever watched the gory process. Using a scalpel he'd found in a first-aid kit inside the lean-to, he removed the head and cold, slimy guts. It was even grosser than he'd expected. Finally, the fish was ready to place on a stone over the fire.

Grateful that the disgusting part was over, he heard another plop. A second fish hit the ground behind him. The drago was already flying away.

Will picked up the new fish and got to work again. Soon, a third landed nearby.

"Three is quite enough," he called after it. "Thank you very much."

His voice woke Opal. She stumbled from the lean-to stretching. She sniffed the air and looked toward the fire.

"Is that fish?"

"It is," Will said, tossing the last cleaned fish next to the two already sizzling.

"Did Bowman catch them?"

"Nope."

"You?"

"He did." Will pointed to the drago, approaching with another fish and yelled, "I told you three was enough."

But the drago didn't fly away, and instead dropped down onto a rock by the fire."

"Is that the drago from New Andrin?" Opal asked.

"I think so," Will said.

"I bet he's the one that almost killed me when we were gliding."

"Could be."

"Is he cold? Why is he in the fire?" Opal stared at the drago now standing in the fire, holding the fish in the flames and nibbling at the darkening flesh.

"I don't know. He's seems pretty heat-tolerant, even for a drago."

"Probably just cold. Weird that he's following us." She took a deep sniff. "I never thought I'd say this about fish for breakfast, but that smells delicious. When will it be ready?"

"The first one should be done in a few minutes."

They turned in unison as branches crackled nearby and Bowman emerged from the bushes, holding a packet of woven leaves. He stopped in his tracks, breathing in the scent of frying fish.

"Here I go searching for breakfast, and you've already got it handled."

Will pointed at the drago. "You can thank him. That drago went fishing for us."

Finished with his meal, the drago took flight and vanished into the sky.

Will noticed the bandage on Bowman's forehead.

"How is it?" he asked.

"Fine," Bowman answered. "Rang my bell pretty good, but just a little headache today."

Bowman joined them next to the fire. He unwrapped the leaf bundles, revealing a pile of wild raspberries.

"Yum!" Will said. "Opal, can you grab a few big ear leaves for plates?"

Opal slipped into the bushes and returned carrying several rigid green leaves shaped like human ears. Will slid the cooked fish onto them. Opal added berries to her "plate," as did Bowman and Will. They devoured the flaky fish and juicy fruit.

The warm food on a cool morning gave them energy and lifted their spirits. Soon, they were tidying the lean-to, packing up, and heading up the trail. With an adult to question, Opal's curiosity kicked into overdrive.

"What's that plant over there? No, the one with the little yellow leaves. Why is it called that? Is that sound a bird or a bug? A frog? What kind? Do the Aellivi eat animals?"

Will tuned her out. He didn't care about the names of things. He was happy just to see all the variety. He'd expected the forest to feel more exotic and was disappointed to find it so similar to Andrin forests. The path they followed was smooth, wide, and free of brush, winding through tall corowood, pine, and oak. Fallen logs, flowering plants, and bushes crowded the forest on either side.

Still, in one important way, this forest felt different. When Will had hiked to waterfalls or picnicked by a stream in Andrin, the forest had just been there. It felt fun if he was having a good time, and dismal if he wasn't. But the trees themselves hadn't offered any feelings.

This forest felt... friendly. Will sensed that it didn't matter whether he was scared, mad, or happy; these trees would feel welcoming and safe. The wind and the trees danced together, the leaves rustling with shared laughter.

And the land couldn't seem to stay still either. Back home the forests were mostly flat with only gentle rises here and there. Hikes in the forest around New Andrin were relaxing. But here the path rose and fell over rolling hills. Climbing up and stomping down made Will's legs ache. Going down was the worst. His shins burned. But then, while climbing, his thighs burned. Maybe uphill was worse. Then downhill again. And so it went. It didn't help that Opal and Bowman chatted away without showing any sign of effort.

The only things that took Will's mind off his legs was the birdsong. Trills echoed all around them, lighter and more intricate than those back home. Will kept peering into the trees, hoping to spot one of the singers, but he could never match a song to a bird. At best, he caught a flash of red, iridescent blue, or yellow. So he matched the colors to the songs.

He was particularly fond of the yellow song. He tried to mimic it, whistling a few notes that were too low. He tried again, a little closer. The runs were hard. He slurred through them and managed a decent imitation. He was rewarded with an answer. Or maybe the bird just chose that moment to sing. Will wanted to believe it was an answer. When the song ended, he tried again, a little better this time.

"That wasn't bad," said a stranger's voice. "But you need more definition on the run, and you were a little flat on that last note."

Will whirled around. Opal and Bowman turned as well.

An Aellivi man stood casually in the path, as if out for a morning stroll. He wore dark brown Aelliven trousers woven from swamp grass fibers, tucked at the knees into soft leather boots. A bright red tunic was cinched at the waist with a wide blue sash. His pale blue eyes and reddish hair were set against light skin, and a tidy goatee made it clear he was an adult, even though he was slightly shorter than Will.

"Roa!" Bowman exclaimed. Bowman bent down to give Roa a big hug.

"You've gotten fat and old," Roa said with a smirk.

Bowman patted his belly. "Desk job. Don't worry, at the rate things are going, I won't have the job or the belly much longer. I'd say you've gotten old, but you haven't."

"Get used to it." Roa said. The Aellivi lived twice as long as the Drin.

The two old friends laughed. Bowman introduced Roa to Opal and Will, and Roa bowed slightly.

"It is an honor to meet you both. I have a boat waiting. Much faster to Acoena by river than forest. Follow me."

He ducked into the bushes.

Will felt instant relief. They wouldn't be hiking anymore. He couldn't wait to let the river do the work. But getting there was its own adventure. When a fallen tree blocked their path, Roa darted up a branch and hopped over as if filled with dragozo. The branches wouldn't hold their weight so Will, Opal, and Bowman had to clamber over awkwardly with grunts. Will felt jealous of Roa. What must it feel like to dance through the forest?

They pushed through a dense thicket. Hearing water gurgling nearby, they scrambled over a series of boulders and emerged onto another path that lead to the riverbank.

Will had seen pictures and done a school report on podders. They were boats shaped like a seedpod, and there was one resting on the muddy bank below. It was built for rapids. Arched supports rose from the wooden frame and met at the top. The tarp roof could be pulled into place over the supports to form a sealed inner compartment. The design allowed it to submerge and pop back to the surface. A weighted bottom made it self-righting.

Will noticed a hatch built into the wooden nose of the boat, perfect for a navigator to pop up and scout ahead, even with the tarp up. At the back, a rudder was positioned where some brave fool would stand, harnessed in, steering blindly based on the navigator's calls.

Will sincerely hoped none of that would be necessary. If the water stayed calm, maybe they could roll down the tarp and enjoy the view.

He admired the scrollwork carved into the lip of the boat, designed to direct splashed water away. He saw no engine and failed to notice the circular oars poking out from small holes running along the side.

Roa led them up a boarding ramp at the rear. Inside, the podder was dark and cool, but enough light filtered through foggy windows for Will to spot the oars. Three seats on each side allowed for six oarsmen. Each seat slid on a short rail for leverage. Will wondered if Roa had a crew waiting nearby.

The tarp roof arched just high enough to shelter anyone seated, provided they were Aellivi. Roa bounded to the front, popped the hatch, and instructed Bowman to take the rudder. Will and Opal sat across from one another.

Opal bent to inspect a harness. "What are these for?"

"You won't need those," Roa assured her. "That's only for rapids with a high risk of capsizing."

Will felt a wave of relief. If they didn't need the harnesses, then surely the ride would be smooth.

Opal sat. "Hey, the seats are just our size," she noted.

"That's why I'm having you row," Roa explained. "You and Will actually fit the equipment. Unlike that monstrosity back there."

Bowman shot his friend a playful scowl.

"You don't have a crew with you?" Will asked, surprised.

"I floated downstream by myself. The four of us should manage just fine getting back."

Accepting his fate, Will sat across from Opal.

The window beside him caught his eye. It wasn't like any he'd seen - green-tinged, veined, and fibrous. Curious, he touched it. The surface was sticky and yielded to his fingers. It wasn't glass at all.

"Isee leaves," Roa explained, catching Will's expression. "Strip the outside layer of the leaf and you're left with a semitransparent, water-resistant, self-adhesive window."

Will marveled at the elegant simplicity. Factory-manufactured flexiglass would've provided a clear, durable view, maybe even a data display. But through the green-tinged haze of the isee leaf, the vines trailing from trees into the river looked mysterious. The water gleamed with a soft, hypnotic shimmer. When this window wore out, you didn't need to order a replacement, you just peeled another leaf.

Will saw something clearly through that window: the most advanced people weren't the one with the most advanced technology, but those who didn't need it at all.

Bowman shoved the podder away from the bank. The slow-moving current caught them drifting sideways toward the center of the river, threatening to spin them downstream.

"Opal, row hard. Now! Bowman, swing us right," Roa shouted.

Opal plunged her oar into the water and pulled with all her strength. Nothing happened.

"Push against the foot pedals too," Roa instructed.

Opal braced her feet against them, dipped the oar again, and pushed while pulling with her arms. A mechanism engaged with a click. The podder shifted, swinging to the right and aligning with the current.

"Will, now you too. We're going backward," Roa called.

Will mimicked Opal's technique. With barely any effort, the podder surged forward. Maybe this trip wouldn't be so bad after all.

They made quick progress despite heading upstream. Will and Opal fell into a rhythm, their strokes matching like the steady beat of a drum. It reminded Will of a song from elementary school. He began humming. Soon they were singing together.

Down the bubbling stream a leaf did float

One brave little ant atop the bobbing boat

His friends had begged him to stay home

But the silly little ant did want to roam.

The ant had many adventures in the song. By the time they'd sung all ten verses and choruses the little ant had journeyed home, older and wiser, and Will didn't think rowing felt so easy anymore. His arms burned. His legs ached. The singing stopped. Then the talking did too. The riverbank drifted by slowly as they worked their way upstream. Will wondered how much farther they had to go.

His thoughts wandered to this morning's dream. Surely there weren't dragons this far south. Still, it lingered in his mind. His dreams always mixed sharp details with strange symbolism. The trick was figuring out which was which. Did it have something to do with the drago? But he seemed friendly and couldn't breathe fire. Maybe the dragon represented some other kind of threat. Something from above.

"Will, stop rowing. Bowman, steer right," Roa called out.

Will gratefully let his oar drop, his arms falling limp into his lap. His thighs throbbed. Through the green-tinted isee leaf window, he saw the river split. They drifted right, dropping into a short run of minor rapids. The turbulence jostled them briefly before the water calmed again.

The branch they followed ran parallel to the main river, but flowed in the opposite direction, downstream. They didn't need to row anymore.

Roa ducked back into the podder and turned a crank. The tarp rolled back along their slender frame supports, letting sunlight pour in. Will basked in the warmth. His aching limbs seemed to relax under the golden light.

"That wasn't so bad, was it?" Roa smiled.

"Kind of," Will replied. "But how does this work? Why is the current going the other way?"

"Aelliven engineering and gravity," Roa answered.

Will felt a shadow cross his face. His dream came rushing back. He looked up. The sun blinded him, just like in the dream. He heard mechanical humming.

"Drone! Cover!" Bowman yelled.

Roa ducked down, closed the hatch, and quickly cranked the podder sides shut. Bowman scrunched under, joining Opal and Will. The humming grew louder.

"What are they doing?" Opal asked. "Did the Aellivi let them bring drones in?"

"I doubt it," said Roa. "They probably thought they could get in and out unnoticed, then beg forgiveness. They just want pictures proving you're here, enough to negotiate your release into their custody. If you're a criminal, we're obligated to turn you over to their authorities."

"Would you do that?"

"If they had proof, I doubt there's anything the council could do to stop it. We honor our treaties, even when our allies don't."

Will heard the accusation behind Roa's words.

The humming grew louder, as if the drone was directly above the podder. No one dared poke their head out to look.

They didn't need to. Moments later, it dropped into view behind them. Bowman splashed water at it. Roa grabbed a spare oar and ducked out the back, swinging wildly. Both men shouted as they tried to knock the drone out of the air, but it slipped just out of reach.

"There's another one!" Will yelled.

The second drone had arms extended, each ending in spinning blades. It zipped toward the podder to saw off the top. The kids ducked to the far side of the boat, scrambling away from the advancing saws. When the drone shifted to the left, they darted right.

Will's dream flashed through his mind. It had offered no solution, only told him that danger came from the sky. He had no idea how to stop it. Their only option was to dive overboard as soon as the roof was gone. He leaned in to tell Opal just as the saw drone peeled back the tarp.

A high-pitched screech split the air.

Emerging from the sun, the red drago plummeted toward the saw drone, hurling it into the water. Sparks flew, and the machine sizzled, and sank. The drago turned on the camera drone, battering it into the water, too.

The threat gone, the red drago fluttered down and landed on the prow of the podder. He stared at them, calm and alert.

"Thank you," Opal whispered.

They watched each other for the rest of the trip. Will sat in silence, deep in thought. The broken camera drone they'd retrieved from the water sat on the bench in front of him, its lifeless eye looking disturbingly human. Roa had fished it out as evidence for a formal complaint. Will wished someone would toss a blanket over it.

They floated silently. The air turned muggy. Before long, Will saw Opal's head loll back, eyes closed. Soon, Will's thoughts faded and sleep overtook him too.

"Bowman. Right."

Will jolted awake at Roa's command. Opal sat up, startled to discover the drago curled in her lap fast asleep. She grinned at Will.

Bowman steered them out of the main current. They skimmed along the riverbank.

Beautifully crafted huts lined the water, their walls and roofs shaped to blend with the surrounding trees and rocks. They looked like natural extensions of the forest. Aellivi men, women, and children walked, played, and worked among the buildings. Their tunics were bright and layered, tied with broad contrasting belts. Most went barefoot, though many adults wore soft boots secured with crisscrossing straps up the calf.

"I always thought Aellivi wore greens and browns like the forest," Will told Roa. "That's how your people are pictured in our children's books."

"We wear the colors of the land, which can be green and brown. But look at the flowers and birds. We wear their colors too."

"Acoena is beautiful. It's so different than I thought it would be."

"This isn't Acoena. It's Owautay, a village on the edge of Acoena."

The river narrowed into a stream, tree branches meeting above them in a leafy tunnel. Ahead, a slender bridge arced across the stream, swaying gently as Aellivi crossed it. The podder drew closer. Will realized the bridge, just wide enough for two to pass, was created by shaping tree branches and vines that stretched across the water. The vines lining the sides served as handrails. He marveled at the elegant, living design as the podder passed beneath.

They drifted on through the leafy tunnel, passing into a more open stretch of water. Will spotted a dark-skinned girl with curly black hair playing at the water's edge, floating a miniature podder on the surface. She couldn't have been more than three feet tall. He waved, and she broke into a wide grin, waving back.

The girl cupped her hands around her mouth and called, "Who did you bring, Roa? Are we having roast Drin for supper tonight?"

Will and Opal's eyes widened. Were they serious?

Roa threw back his head and laughed. "Not this time, Liwan," he called. "Besides, these two are a little scrawny. Hardly worth the trouble."

Liwan trotted alongside the bank, keeping up with them easily. She tilted her head, pretending to study them critically.

"I suppose," she said. "They look like they'd be tender, but maybe they're tougher than they appear." She wrinkled her nose playfully. "Did they rip the roof off your podder when you caught them?"

Will and Opal shared a worried glance. Roa noticed and laughed even harder.

"Don't worry, little sprouts," he said. "We haven't eaten Drin in... oh, at least a few years."

Liwan grinned mischievously and skipped away down the bank, her laughter trailing behind her.

The podder rounded a bend and the river opened into Lake Acoena. A bustling wharf came into view, nestled among white boulders and sprawling oak trees. The city climbed the valley from the water's edge, spreading into the foothills. Every house was white or tan. A massive palace glistened at the summit, its bright banners fluttering in the sun. It took Will's breath away.

"This is Acoena," Roa said reverently.

The drago stirred. Instead of flying off as Will expected, it hopped onto Opal's shoulder and curled its tail gently around her neck.

"Looks like you have a friend," Bowman said.

Opal smiled and cautiously offered her hand. The drago sniffed it, and she began to stroke its head.

"What should I call you," she murmured.

Roa guided the podder to the dock where workers waited. They pointed at the damaged boat, clearly curious about the torn-up roof.

Will stepped out and instinctively looked at the sky.

"They wouldn't dare send a drone to the capital," Roa assured him.

Will gave a nervous smile, hoping he was right.

He felt a tug on his sleeve. The girl from the riverbank peered up at him with large, curious eyes.

"I'm Liwan. What's your name?"

"I'm Will. And she's Opal."

"Nice to meet you, Will," Liwan said warmly. "Don't worry. We don't really eat Drin." She turned her wide smile toward Opal. "Cali's beautiful, Opal."

Will studied her. Liwan looked like a toddler, but her speech and manner made it clear she wasn't as young as she seemed. Will realized it might take some time to adjust to the small folk.

"Thank you," Opal said, then glanced at the drago on her shoulder. "Is Cali its name? How do you know?

"He told me." Liwan answered matter-of-factly. "Did you know he's a blood dragon?"

"I didn't even know he was a he, for sure?"

A hush rippled across the wharf. Workers stepped aside as a regal woman approached, flanked by guards. She moved with quiet authority, her long tunic flowing like water around her legs. Her gown shimmered with fine embroidery, and her white hair streamed down her back like a banner.

Will's gaze caught on her eyes, striking and pale, like gemstones catching sunlight. He realized with a jolt she was his height, and she was looking directly at him.

Roa bowed low.

The woman gave a shallow nod, her attention drifting to the damaged podder.

"We are glad to have you back, Roa, and in one piece," she said, voice calm but steely.

Roa straightened. "Andrin sent drones into Aelliviss."

Her face darkened. "That will not stand."

She gestured to a guard, who immediately moved to retrieve the wreckage.

"Your Highness," Roa said "may I present my foster-brother Gale Bow-man. This young woman is Opal, and this is Will. My Andrin friends, this is Queen Areu."

Will froze as the queen's gaze returned to him. He wasn't sure what to say. Was he supposed to bow?

She stepped closer.

"Come," said Queen Areu. "The council is waiting. There is much to be done."

The guards moved in formation, one now holding the ruined drone. Roa and Bowman followed the queen, answering Opal's flurry of questions. Will hung back, a few steps behind them.

Then Queen Areu slowed. Without a word, she slipped her arm through his. She leaned in, her breath warm against his ear.

"Welcome, Will." She whispered. "We've been waiting for you... a very long time."

23

JUST BREATHE

Acoena was certainly different from New Andrin. There were no gleaming skyscrapers, no cars speeding along roadways. The city filled the entire valley, though much of it was hidden beneath ancient trees. The wide, central boulevard where Opal walked with the queen's party, alongside hundreds of other pedestrians, led to a gleaming white palace on the hill. The buildings were dazzling white.

As they walked, Opal noticed a pattern. Each section of the city had a large park, bordered by businesses and surrounded by homes. It created neighborhoods where everything was within walking distance. It was far more efficient than the scattershot sprawl of New Andrin.

The colors of the grass, trees, banners, and clothing appeared almost fluorescent against the gleaming buildings. Though the city was packed with people, only human voices and birdsong floated through the air. No mechanical hum, no traffic, no chaos.

Everyone was well dressed in bright colors. No one looked hungry, homeless, or even sad.

There was so much to take in; the colors, the smells, the music, the way the locals moved with effortless grace. Opal felt like a clumsy giant, especially around the tiny children.

Queen Areu made her uneasy. She was stunning, but her eyes were spooky. They changed color when she spoke. That, and the whole "being royalty" thing. Still, Opal felt a flicker of pride that the queen had come to greet her personally. She imagined they were being led to a banquet hall to feast and celebrate her arrival. It bothered her a little that the queen seemed more focused on Will. Wasn't she the one that was going to save them?

The queen's guards led the way, laughing and chatting. They didn't seem worried about security. No one bowed or stared. People moved around the queen as if she were just another citizen, though children openly gawked at the Drin visitors. Most of the attention was on Opal, thanks to the drago perched on her shoulder, its tail still curled securely around her neck.

Once when the queen stopped to speak with a woman, a little girl shyly approached Bowman. She was less than three feet tall and held out a tiny bouquet of sweet alyssum. Bowman took it gently, the whole bunch fitting between his thumb and forefinger. He brought it to his nose and inhaled deeply.

"Thank you, little one," he said. "They smell wonderful. They're beautiful, and so are you!"

The girl giggled and ran to hide behind her mother. Opal smiled and waved. The girl peeked out, then ducked back into hiding.

About fifteen minutes later, they reached the valley's edge and began climbing toward the castle. There were fewer buildings and people, and more orchards and fields. Opal now walked beside the queen.

At a crossroads, a young man leaned against a tree, smoking a long, thin pipe. His tunic was bright orange, his leggings dark red, and he wore no shoes. Long, dark hair flopped over his eyes. He looked like the New Andrin university students who hung out at the downtown cafés, blowing colored smoke and trying to look profound. Queen Areu stopped to greet him.

"Good afternoon, Hwue. I've brought your student."

Hwue pushed away from the tree and looked up at Opal, studying her. "All right, then," he said. "We'd best get started. Let's go, Opal."

Opal turned to Queen Areu. "I thought we were going to the council."

"We are," the queen replied with a smile, "but you have other work to do. Go with Hwue. We'll see you again soon."

And with that, the queen and everyone Opal knew within a thousand miles walked away.

She was grateful when Will ran back and hugged her. "Don't worry," he whispered. "I trust them. You'll be okay."

Tears sprang to her eyes as he ran to catch up to the queen. She hoped he was right.

Hwue was knocking the ash out of his pipe. She couldn't believe this kid was going to be her teacher.

"How old are you?" she asked.

"Fifty-one."

She blinked. Hwue looked like a teenager, yet he was apparently older than her father. Aellivi, with their longer life span, aged differently. She knew that, but still.

"Are you a teacher?"

"When I need to be."

"What do you teach?"

"Nothing."

"Then why am I here?"

"To learn something."

"That doesn't make any sense."

He flipped his hair out of his eyes. "Come along."

She gave up. They walked in silence until Hwue veered off the path, pushing aside some large leaves and leading her through underbrush to a pond.

"Cali will need to stay with me," he said.

As if on cue, Cali unwrapped himself from her neck and hopped onto Hwue's arm. The loss stung, but Opal didn't protest. Hwue pointed to a large flat rock near the pond's edge.

"Sit there."

She did.

"I'll be back when you have learned. When you see."

"Learned what? See what? What am I supposed to study?"

"Do not leave the rock," he said, ignoring her questions. "Except to, you know. You can do that behind that bush. Morning swims are allowed. I'd stay out of the water in the afternoon when the pickle leeches are feeding. Otherwise, stay on the rock."

"And do what?"

"Breathe."

Hwue instructed her to take deep, rapid breaths and saturate herself with oxygen. Once she'd done that, breathing would no longer be necessary... until it was, at which point she would start again. He told her she could do this any time she was bored.

He then turned and disappeared into the underbrush with Cali now firmly wrapped around his neck. The drago gave Opal a farewell chirp.

Opal sat fuming. She was hungry. She was tired. She was dirty. She'd expected to be welcomed, fed, maybe allowed to rest after the chaos of the last few days. Instead, she was alone on a rock in the middle of the forest, told to breathe, as if she could do anything but breathe.

Frustration churned into defiance. Maybe it was all a test. Maybe she was supposed to march into the council chamber and prove she was brave and clever and not someone to sideline on a stone. Maybe the Aellivi didn't actually have a solution and had stuck her out here to keep her from figuring that out.

Eventually, she even got bored of being angry. Her mind drifted, replaying the events of the last few days, then memories from years ago, until all those thoughts grew dull. She groaned.

She was so bored. There was nothing to do. Nothing to see.

That's when she remembered her instructions. Breathe when you're bored.

She sat up straighter and began breathing deeply, feeling her belly and chest rise and fall. Over and over. Finally, she let her breath out and sat in stillness. Warmth from the sun-soaked rock slid into her body. The buzzing insects faded as a new buzzing filled her ears. Her hands tingled. Her whole body seemed to vibrate.

She didn't know how long she sat without breathing, longer than she thought possible. A sense of calm overtook her. Time slipped past. The forest grew beautiful, not because it had changed, but because she had. When her body felt a hunger for air, she began to breathe again. What had just happened?

As the sun dropped lower, the world shifted. Insects danced above the pond. A fish leapt up and snatched one out of the air. A young doe emerged across the water, ears twitching, nose raised to the wind, before dipping her head to drink. For a while, Opal was entertained.

Then the sun disappeared and darkness came fast.

Rustling filled the trees, and her imagination ran wild. Where was Hwue? Had they really left her here overnight? Was that a growl? Her first instinct was to get up, leave, go find someone. But where would she go? She didn't know the path. The dark made the forest unfamiliar. The best plan, for now, was to stay put.

The growl returned, but this time she realized it was her stomach. And she was cold. She stood up to get her blood moving and quickly realized she had to pee. She peered into the darkness and wished she'd gone earlier.

Arms stretched in front of her, she crept into the brush, trying to avoid face-slapping branches. She found what might have been the bush Hwue pointed to and did her business, then stumbled back through the dark.

Her rock, like so many in the valley, was white. It glowed faintly in the starlight, guiding her way. When she reached it, she stopped in surprise. A cloth bag now sat on the rock. Inside, she found a blanket, a flask of water, and a leaf packet holding two berry-and-nut biscuits and a sandwich.

She couldn't see what was in the sandwich, but it smelled delicious: sharp and savory, warm and earthy. Cheese and onion, for sure. The rest was a mystery. Whatever it was, it disappeared fast. She drank from the flask and ate one biscuit, saving the other just in case. She didn't know when more food would come.

Opal rolled the bag into a pillow, wrapped herself in the blanket, and lay down. Rustling still echoed from the trees, but she felt better now. Someone was watching. Someone had brought food. Someone wouldn't let the animals eat her.

She stared up at the stars. Somehow they seemed even brighter here than they had on the Andrin prairie. She wondered if her dad was looking at the stars too. She hoped he was okay. She missed the silly poems he used to write for her. She missed his arms wrapping tightly around her. When he held her, nothing in the world could touch her.

She blinked against the tears threatening to fall.

She sat up and did more of the deep breathing Hwue had taught her. After, her breathing became slow, deep and deliberate. Her thoughts settled.

And then, at last, she fell into a deep, dreamless sleep.

***

From a broad branch above, Hwue watched her. He was alone, having sent Cali to find Will.

It was too early for any true progress, but he was pleased. She had moved past anger, past confusion, and found sleep. That was something.

He hadn't been sure about this plan when the council revived Oesca's Course. It had been centuries since anyone had attempted such a training, let alone rushed it as he'd been asked to do.

And the student?

A Drin.

Could a Drin even manage what was required?

Hwue didn't know, but he would try everything. Because if she couldn't... if Opal couldn't master what the Aellivi had to teach, then life as they all knew it would end.

Not just in the Aelliven forest.

Everywhere.

24

WHAT REMAINS

Biriad loped up the dark hillside on all fours, feeling powerful in the crisp northern air. Free. Flint waited below. Biriad was tempted to kill him now, but there was much more to gain by being patient. From the top of the ridge, he surveyed the valley they would need to cross to reach Varsik Castle. A wide river cut through the center. The castle clung to the side of a mountain, looking small, cold, and dead in the dim moonlight. The valley offered little cover from dragons. He scanned the sky, then turned back to tell Flint the way was clear.

Biriad resented Flint. His body was weak even if power flowed through it. True, Flint had known how to disable the sonic fences to give them access to this valley, but he couldn't see in the dark or run long distances. Biriad could rip him apart with the flick of a claw. What they found at Varsik Castle would determine how much longer Flint remained useful. If the castle was in ruins, Biriad would kill Flint and strike out on his own. But if it provided a stronghold from which Flint could command armies, Biriad would wait. Let Flint consolidate power. Then destroy him and take his place. For now, only the promise of greater power and more victims kept Flint alive.

They crossed the valley without spotting any dragons. As the sun rose, it painted the mountains in gold and cast brilliant light across Varsik Castle. It wasn't a ruin. It stood unbreached and whole.

Golden light spilled across Flint's face, his expression rapturous.

Biriad's eye caught movement. Miles away, a small black shape flapped across a distant mountain peak.

"Dragon," Biriad warned.

Flint closed his eyes and muttered a casting. Nothing obvious happened, but Biriad wasn't sure what to expect. Flint finished, smiled, reached for Biriad, and began another casting.

A snap. A lurch. The world bent sideways.

Biriad snarled, claws digging into stone as he landed on solid ground. They were no longer on the hillside, but atop the castle wall. The valley sprawled behind him, miles away.

He crouched low, lips peeled back, scanning the sky and sniffing the air, making sure no threat had followed.

***

With Biriad off assessing the castle, Flint began his own exploration. Dirt filled the cracks between the stone walls. Weeds and lichen clung to every surface. Loose stones littered the walkway, but the damage was largely cosmetic. Once he had an army, repairs would be simple. He glanced at the sky. The dragon still circled in the distance. As long as the Drin had to worry about dragons, few would join him. He would have to deal with the threat from above. But first, the King's Hall.

He'd studied blueprints and diagrams of Varsik Castle for years. His feet found the path as if remembering it from another life. Down a spiral stairway into the grand hall, empty except for old tapestries, through the dining room, where chairs stood askew as if their occupants had just risen from a meal, and into the castle's massive entryway. Each room was cloaked in dirt and preserved in the exact state it had been left when Alberoth led his army south.

Flint's footsteps echoed in the rafters.

The entryway opened into another large hall. To the left, the castle's two-foot-thick defensive doors were gone, the iron hinges twisted, the drawbridge exposed. To the right, the burned and broken doors of the King's Hall remained in place, warped but mostly intact.

Light filtered through narrow windows on either side of the King's Hall. From the entryway, Flint could make out few details. His heart pounded. He stepped forward slowly, afraid of what he might find. His eyes adjusted. Statues stood in their alcoves. Light streamed through shattered panes above the throne.

He stepped closer, breath tight in his chest.

Long before anyone knew of his ambitions, Alberoth had commissioned an Aelliven magi to grow a throne from a tree, right here in this hall. The Living Throne of Power. They had shaped the throne from its living trunk. It was said the wood molded itself to its ruler. Smooth as silk. Alive with power.

Now, he saw only destruction. Flint imagined the dragons' rage upon returning from war. Perhaps they'd ripped the gates off. Perhaps one had blasted the inner doors with fire, then shattered them with a swing of his tail. Once inside, he would have filled the room with his massive bulk and reduced the throne to cinders. Then, the dragons had fled north, away from humans. Away from death.

Flint stood before the wreckage; his knees weak. The Living Throne of Power was gone. Charred, hollowed out, nothing but ash.

This was supposed to be his inheritance. He had dreamed of sitting there and feeling the magic rise up through his spine, confirming what he had always believed: that power ran in his blood. That destiny bent toward him.

He clenched his fists and stared at the ruin, struggling to contain the scream rising in his throat. The throne was gone. He was a ruler without a crown. A king of ash.

The door behind the throne was also charred. It crumbled when he touched it. The hallway beyond was dark. Flint reeled off another casting and an orb of yellow light floated above him, lighting his way. The passage beyond was untouched by fire. Portraits and tapestries lined the walls. He counted doors. At the end of the hall, he found the one he hoped for.

If this room was gone too, he had nothing left.

He held his breath and pushed it open.

A sharp gasp escaped him.

It was here. It was all here.

Alberoth's library, untouched by flame, was sealed in time by powerful preservation magic. Books filled the walls, floor to ceiling, thirty feet high. One section contained loosely rolled scrolls. A long table overflowed with parchments. It would take lifetimes to absorb this much knowledge.

Flint stepped inside, his heart pounding.

The throne may have burned. The dragons may have shattered his symbol of rule. But this... this was the mind of Alberoth. Somewhere in this room might be the castings used to bend Biriad to Alberoth's will. There would be castings to help him win over the Dragon Lords. Then the people of Andrin would fall in line. The Cavrik would follow. The Aellivi, in time, would kneel.

The loss of the throne no longer stung.

Flint let out a slow, ragged breath, a grin spreading across his face.

And through these ancient pages, the world would know him not as a madman, murderer, or mage, but as the architect of a new age.

25

EVERYTHING IS ALIVE

A sliver of light broke through the trees and fell across Opal's eyelids, rousing her. She lifted her head and felt pain rocket down her spine. The rock had not made a comfortable bed. The blanket fell into her lap as she sat up and rubbed her eyes. White mist drifted above the still pond. Birds twittered, starting the day off with song.

Another packet of leaves had been left on the rock. Opal opened it and devoured the berries and oatcake inside. Now knowing she would be fed, she crumbled last night's stale biscuit and tossed it on the water for the fish. After a quick trip to the toilet bush, she returned, wondering how much longer she'd be stuck here.

The water looked cold and the air wasn't much warmer. Still, she hadn't had a bath in days. She laid her clothes on the rock and carefully dipped one foot in.

"Brrrrrr!"

It was freezing. But she had already started, and the need to feel clean outweighed the discomfort. She held her foot back in place, adjusting to the temperature. Then the other foot. Soon she was wading deeper, splashing water on her face and head. Her toes were already going numb. She changed her mind about swimming and scrubbed quickly, dashing out and using her clothes to dry off before putting them back on. Despite shivering, she realized she felt great. The cold water had done its job. She was wide awake.

By the time the sun shone directly overhead, her anger had returned. It was all so stupid. Just her, on this rock, with nothing happening and nothing to do. What was there to learn? Again she toyed with the idea of leaving, but the Aelliven forest still frightened her a little. So she stayed, lying on the rock and breathing. The stillness when she stopped her breath became an eternity. Hours passed in a soft buzz of contentment.

The sun was nearing the edge of the trees when she realized she hadn't moved for most of the day, yet it felt like she'd just sat down. Soon it would be dark. Meals always arrived just as she felt hunger. It was both comforting and maddening to know she was being watched. She decided she'd stay as long as food kept appearing.

She stood, stretched, and jogged in place to warm up. It looked like she'd be spending another night on the rock.

Days passed like this: wake, eat, bathe, sit, breathe, eat, sleep. On and on, cycling through boredom, anger, frustration, and acceptance. She lost track of how many days she'd been there. Maybe a week. Maybe more.

One day, afraid she was forgetting who she was, she quietly whispered her name. Her voice sounded like a clanging gong. She didn't speak again.

In the midst of one of her breathing meditations, a fat worm crawled across her rock. While not breathing, she gently placed her finger in its path. The worm climbed aboard. It was green, about two inches long, with a pair of legs on each wriggling segment. It's face was dominated by two large eyes, four waggling antennae, and a wide, straight mouth. The worm lifted the front half of its body and weaved in the air.

Opal smiled. They weren't so different. Just two creatures exploring the world. She set the worm down gently. It rippled away, stopped on a branch, turned to look at her, then vanished into the leaves.

A trail of ants caught her eye, marching along a branch carrying leaves and sticks. She followed their route to a mound where they disappeared. More ants streamed up and out. She watched their coordination, how they resolved collisions with a flick of antennae. They reminded her of New Andrin commuters.

Next came the pixie flies. Not truly pixies, not truly flies, but they seemed like both. Three inches long, with oversized black eyes and shimmering wings, they skimmed the pond. Their front claw-like arms were folded in front of them, but unfolded to dip into the water to gather algae.

She watched in awe, until a silver fish burst from the water, swallowing a pixie fly. Sadness hit her. But the fly had also eaten algae. Why didn't she mourn for the algae?

A bird plunged from the sky, slicing into the water, catching a fish in its beak and swallowing it whole.

Opal inhaled deeply, filling her body with oxygen then returned to stillness.

She blinked. The pond, the trees, the air - it all glowed. Connected. Alive. Powered by the same source.

She jumped off the rock and felt a shock jolt up her leg. Looking down, she saw the crushed body of a worm. Her heart sank. Was it the one she'd met earlier? Threads connecting it to the web of life shimmered and snapped. She felt it.

Ants rushed in and carried it away. It was food for the colony.

And Opal understood: Death did not exist. The energy would transfer. It always did. Everything: rock, tree, insect, soil, water, air... all related. One thing in infinite forms. Even atoms, she remembered, vibrated in relation to one another. They were aware. Alive, in their own way.

She stood transfixed. The world pulsed with life and awareness.

We're alive, she thought.

Everything is alive. There is nothing else.

She expanded beyond her body. Energy flowed through her. And joy. She was an atom. She was the universe. She wasn't alone. She would never be alone.

She threw her head back and laughed. The sound echoed up to the stars.

26

WAKING DREAMS

Will sat alone at a table on the edge of the square, quietly waiting for Liwan. Music drifted through the square, families picnicked on the grass, and children laughed as they chased one another. Everything peaceful. Everything perfect.

He couldn't believe he felt so at home here after just a couple of weeks. After Queen Areu sent Opal off with Hwue, the rest of their group had walked to a small white stone house, where Liwan stood waiting.

"Will, I believe you met Liwan at the wharf," the queen said. "She will be your teacher and host during your stay here."

Liwan, the "little girl" Will had first seen playing with a miniature podder, turned out to be no child at all. She was around twenty in Drin years and had been studying the effects of current and wind on river navigation for her water pilot's test.

Liwan smiled, warm and welcoming. The queen left with the rest of her party. Bowman lingered.

"I'll see you soon, alright?" he said, then jogged to catch up with the others heading to the palace.

Will ducked through Liwan's doorway. Her little house was cozy and full of plants, with windows overlooking the street. His bedroom was tiny and his bed barely looked big enough. He thought he might have to sleep diagonally.

Once they were settled, Will asked about the queen's comment, that they had been waiting for him.

Liwan explained that several Aellivi diviners had foretold the arrival of a Drin boy with an echo of Aelliven blood and the gift of dream sight. He would be trained like one of them to bring wisdom to the Drin. Will, they believed, was that boy.

In the days that followed, Will's dreams became calm. He no longer feared going to sleep. In the mornings, he shared his dreams with Liwan. For the first time, someone understood. They tried different methods of divination, but none seemed to fit. Will found pendulums creepy, cards too random, and bone tossing absurd.

Liwan reassured him. "There's no magic in the objects. The magic is in your mind. They're just tools. The trick is finding the one that works for you."

That part made sense. It was similar to what their teacher had told the class before Opal summoned the karuk. He'd said there was no power in the words of a casting, only power in the caster. In the same way, Will's dreams meant nothing unless he could understand them.

Afternoons were spent in the classroom. At first, he hated it. None of the desks fit, so he sat on the floor in the back, feeling awkward. But the other students made a point to include him at recess. Soon, he had many friends, and no longer minded his size.

He learned Maellogi, and studied Aelliven philosophy, history, and worldview. The Drin had always been the center of his education; now he saw through another lens. It was disorienting. It was also thrilling.

Liwan had become Will's teacher, companion, and friend. One evening, sipping cocoa in Liwan's kitchen, they talked.

"You have been taught your whole life that you are here," Liwan said, tapping Will's forehead. "And I live in here." She tapped her own. "You're not wrong. But... think of it this way: when I lived in West Doyova, I found your InfoMax fascinating. You've built something that mimics how our minds work."

She blew on her cocoa, then continued. "You're like a logicomp with your own hard drive and processor. Smart. Powerful. But when connected to the InfoMax, you become a super logicomp with access to all the other drives, all their information. That's what it's like when your mind connects to the network."

"So my dreams are like downloads from other logicomps?"

"Exactly. Your brain has a better receiver than most Drin. You connect in sleep. But your conscious mind doesn't believe it's possible, so you lose the connection when you wake."

"How do I stay connected?"

"Train you waking mind to ask, 'Am I dreaming?' Eventually you'll do that while dreaming. You'll become aware you're dreaming. The first few times, you'll be so excited you wake up, but eventually, once you awake in a dream, you will be able to control it."

"Cool," Will said.

"When you master that, you'll be able to cross the boundary any time you need to and access the network while awake."

The first time it worked, he was dreaming that he and Opal were running from mukdri, their growls and slurps echoing behind them. Mud clung to his feet, creeping upward. He felt it crawling into his skin. He was becoming one of them. Terror paralyzed him.

Then a thought broke through: Am I dreaming?

The world around him wavered. Gray mist and shifting forms.

It felt unreal and he knew he was asleep.

The mukdri dissolved.

He laughed aloud, then woke, gasping. He'd done it. He'd been aware inside the dream. It hadn't lasted, but it had begun.

The days settled into rhythm: dream work, study, supper, reflection. Will almost forgot the reason he was here. When thoughts of Biriad surfaced, he had pushed them aside.

Here, having supper with his Aellivi friends, he was safe. No need to think about monsters.

Bubbles of light floated overhead in constant motion, never drifting beyond the square. Will didn't understand how they worked. He assumed it was magic. On the stage, performers spun in a traditional Aelliven dance, long strips of cloth streaming behind them in colorful blurs.

Liwan navigated the crowd with ease, balancing several plates, bowls, and a mug in her tiny arms. Will was constantly amazed at how much food the Aellivi ate.

Each night, the community gathered in the square to share music, dance, stories, and food. At first, Will had found the gatherings loud and overwhelming, but within days, he'd come to love them. He would miss them back in Andrin.

Liwan reached the table, put down her haul, and sat down across from Will. In unison, they touched their hands to forehead and heart, closed their eyes, and said, "For life, I give thanks." The Aellivi did this before every meal, honoring the life that would nourish them. They dug in, enjoying their food as the dancers whirled.

Scanning the food stalls, Will spotted Hwue with Opal beside him. He wondered if he was dreaming. Then, without thinking Will jumped to his feet and shouted, "Opal!"

Seeing him approach, Opal stopped in her tracks. For a split second, her smile flickered, like she was unsure if he was real, too. Then her face lit up with full, blazing joy. She ran to him, and they collided in a hug so fierce it nearly knocked him over.

"Will," she whispered, her voice shaking.

He pulled back, studying her face. "Are you okay?"

Opal's eyes shone, but her gaze drifted upward toward the glowing orbs overhead, then to the dancers on stage. "Yeah," she said. "I think I'm... better than okay."

A laugh bubbled out of her, strange and wild and free.

"What's so funny?" Will asked, pulling back.

"You," she said, grinning. "Me. Us. All of it. It's just..." She twirled in time to the music.

Hwue leaned in close to Will's ear. "Don't worry. She's just figured some things out. It'll take time to soak in. She'll be back to herself soon."

Will hoped Hwue was right. Opal didn't seem hurt, just... changed.

She looked at him as if reading his thoughts.

"We're gonna be okay. We will. But we're not the same, Will. Not anymore."

27

THE LEASH

Stone sat on the balcony of his hotel room, watching the sun set over the plains and distant rocky peaks of the Northern Realms. A week ago, he'd never heard of this backwater known as Hillside. A few weeks ago, he'd been locked in a prison cell just up the row from Flint. He was grateful to be free of the dungeon, but now felt imprisoned by the compulsion that drove him north, and straight into this strange little town.

Hillside had been built on the largest of the rocky hills in the area. There was one hotel, a two-story brick eyesore at the top, overlooking the disorganized town below. Even from his high vantage point, it was hard to trace a direct route through its maze of winding streets.

The hotel was decades out of date, but Stone didn't mind. It beat the concrete box he'd been in. He'd thought the karuk would kill them all that day. The thing had walked right past his cell like he wasn't even there, focused solely on Flint.

It shouldn't have surprised him. Of course, the karuk was drawn to the most powerful mage in the dungeon's Magic Suppression Wing. If a nightmare beast like that was searching for someone, Flint would be the obvious choice.

Stone's gift was unique, but hardly worthy of notice by something like a karuk. He could steal without touching a thing. With a coin in his palm, he could pull nearby gold like a magnet. There were no break-ins, no fingerprints. Just vanishing valuables. It made him hard to catch. Eventually, security footage outed him. He'd served five years of a ten-year sentence. The state had tried to rehabilitate him, and he'd played along, but stealing was still easier than working.

Since Flint had broken them out, Stone had stuck to low-surveillance areas and stealing nondescript valuables. Just enough to live on, nothing flashy. He had no intention of joining Flint's cult of personality, even as he was drawn towards him. Flint had made it clear there'd be consequences for those who refused to follow, but so far, Stone was doing just fine on his own.

He propped his feet on the balcony railing and watched the sky blaze with oranges and pinks. Sunsets used to soothe him. Now they triggered dread. Night meant sleep. And sleep meant dreams.

Last night's had been the worst yet.

He'd been running through Hillside's twisting streets, chased by Repticin with glittering eyes, scaly skin, and razored claws just feet behind him. He turned a corner and hit a brick wall. There was no way out.

"Stone," a voice had said softly.

Flint. He was always in these dreams. In this one, he was leaning from a window, arm outstretched, offering safety. Stone grasped his hand. Flint's face changed. His eyes blackened and mouth twisted. Stone tried to let go and drop, but Flint's grip only tightened.

He'd woken, retching over the side of his bed, stomach clenching with fear that never let up.

The sun gone, he went into his room, clicked through the vidscreen channels, searching for anything to drown the anxiety. He settled on an old sitcom about an Aellivi trying to adjust to Drin life. It was dumb, but it made him chuckle. Maybe he just needed food.

The ground beef sandwich arrived, and he devoured it in bed. He'd just swallowed the last bite when he heard screaming.

And then, gunshots.

He leapt from the bed and raced to the balcony.

Below, Hillside was chaos.

People tore through the streets, primal wolves in pursuit. Stone watched in horror as the hulking wolves crushed victims in their jaws, tore through doors, dragging screaming residents into the night. A woman clutching a young child pounded on a shop door, before being yanked into the darkness, shrieking.

Then... a fist pounded on his door.

"We're evacuating the hotel! Come to the lobby."

Stone didn't move. His eyes locked on something rising from the shadows. Something tall, hulking, familiar. The karuk.

It lunged from the dark, arms outstretched, and dragged a fleeing man into its deadly embrace.

Stone had survived the karuk once; he wasn't sure he'd be so lucky a second time. He bolted. Down the stairs. Into the lobby. Out to the street. Onto a bus.

The roads weren't safe, but they were better than staying in town. The bus threaded its way out of Hillside, lights off. Through the windows, Stone caught glimpses of horrors he would never forget, like a woman running, a flash of fur, a scream swallowed by the dark.

Once out of town, a caravan of fleeing vehicles drove through the night, winding their way through darkness. Everyone in Stone's bus remained silent. No one asked where the bus was heading or seemed to care. They were just happy to be moving away from Hillside and death.

By dawn, the terrain was no longer passable. Passengers stumbled out, bleary and shaken. Hundreds of people, stunned, were herded forward. The only way left was north, up the valley.

Stone trudged with them over rocky terrain up the mountainside. Then he saw it, rising just ahead.

The castle.

The same one from his dreams.

The same one where Flint now stood on the wall, arms raised in welcome.

The dreams weren't warnings. They were a leash.

Stone stopped walking. Bent over. And vomited.

28

Becoming a Magi

O pal was happy to see Will. She marveled at the light flowing through him. He was a remarkable boy. How had she not seen it when they first met?

Returning to Acoena overwhelmed her. Threads of connection shimmered everywhere; families, friends, pets, birds feasting on crumbs, insects doing the same. Music and dance vibrated, making everything pulse with energy. She couldn't stop taking it all in, yet couldn't process it all. A nice, quiet supper at home might have been easier on her senses. She didn't know yet that Aellivi families didn't eat nice, quiet suppers at home.

After that chaotic night, she settled in and began her magic studies with Hwue. At first, they focused on learning Maellogi. Hwue started with verbs, then nouns, and then pronouns. Her head ached from all the tenses and forms, but after a month she began to grasp the ancient language.

One afternoon, they sat beneath a tree outside Hwue's house. Opal was reading a passage written four thousand years ago when she came across a familiar-looking word: biriadi.

"It's the word from which the karuk draws his name," Hwue explained. "Biriadi means fear."

"So, I unleashed fear."

"You did. And there's no mystery why you had the power. Tell me, how did you feel that day?"

"I was angry."

"Why?"

"Because I had to attend Pascam and be a mage instead of becoming an engineer and going to space."

"You were afraid."

"No," she insisted. "I was angry."

"Think it through," Hwue said patiently. "You were afraid that the life you wanted was over, afraid you would be unhappy forever. And from that fear, anger grew."

Opal was quiet. "I guess I was afraid," she admitted. "Scared no one would like me. Scared to be called up in the front of the class and shamed."

"Exactly. Fear ran through you and meshed with the magical power you were born with. It's unfortunate that you landed on that page, because when you called Biriad by name, with the fear in you, it was impossible not to bring him forth."

"If Biriad is fear, can't I just be brave to get rid of him?"

Hwue laughed. "If only it were that easy. Bravery isn't the opposite of fear."

"Then what is?"

"That's something you'll have to discover."

Two months in, the Maellogi started to sink in. Some words felt natural. When the Aellivi spoke among themselves, she could follow along, even if their dialect differed from the ancient texts.

One day, after wrestling with a difficult casting, Opal took a break and asked Hwue a question she'd been holding onto.

"Why do you call your magicians magi, but the Drin are mages?"

Hwue smiled. "It's sort of an insult."

"What? Why?"

"Break the word down. Maellogi has three parts. 'Ma' means this world and all its life. 'Ell' is the ancient form of 'word.' 'Ogi' refers to the act of speaking. So Maellogi means something like 'life-word-speaking.'"

"So 'ma' would mean all life. But what's the difference between 'ge' and 'gi'? I assume it's a variation on the same meaning."

"Yes, 'ma' means life. But gi implies balance, give and take. Ge implies one who takes without giving."

"You think we're thieves?" Her eyes narrowed. "How nice."

"The Drin use life's power for greed and desire," Hwue said calmly. "You don't dwell within life. You see yourselves as outside it and exploit life without thought."

Opal frowned. The Aellivi had seemed so welcoming. Now she wasn't so sure.

"You're training me to be a mage and insulting me at the same time?"

"No. We hope you'll become a Drin magi. A life-dweller. A teacher."

"You've been calling us names for centuries. Did that make you feel good?"

"After Belken? Yeah. Every single time," Hwue chuckled.

Opal laughed. She could see his point, though she still felt a flicker of shame for the Drin. She wondered what the teachers at Pascam would think, knowing they'd been mocked in the very language they taught.

"There are no Drin magi?" she asked.

"There is one who lives and works on Vulkera, the dragon nursery isle," Hwue said. "Used to be a powerful magi, but she lives in the ash fields now."

A Drin magi. She didn't know why that idea stirred something in her chest. Another Drin who had walked the path she had. It gave her a strange sense of comfort.

Weeks later, she made another discovery. She was translating castings into Andrin when she rushed outside to find Hwue.

"It's poetry!" she shouted. "Castings are poems!"

"They are," Hwue said without looking up.

"But why poems? Why not just say what you mean?"

"Because poetry is the language of emotion. Words carry power, but when they're charged with feeling, they connect to the source of life."

He flipped through the casting book and handed it to her. "Read this one."

She hesitated.

"You're ready," he said.

She read the title; *A Fasis Bloom Grows*. That didn't sound too danger-ous.

She read aloud. The words flowed effortlessly, painting vivid images of flowers blooming, connected to life, reaching for the light.

She reached the final stanza.

"Aluea dua somahtisa, dasua polemitus arsum fasis."

A sprout pushed through the soil. It grew, stretched, and bloomed, orange and pink petals unfurling. Opal gasped. Hwue beamed.

"How do you feel?"

"Incredible."

"And your body?"

She checked in. "Tired."

"As it should. The emotion and words channeled your energy outward. Eventually, you'll learn to draw from other sources when needed, but for now, you are limited to what's in you. That's why we eat so much. And nap. A lot."

He disappeared into his house and returned with peaches and another book.

"Try this one. Then we'll eat."

Opal looked at the title: *A Flame in the Darkness*. It was a two-line casting. She pronounced the words easily. A tiny flame flickered on her fingertip.

"Memorize it," Hwue said. "You'll never be in the dark again." He spoke a few Maellogi words and the flame vanished. "And keep the book. It's yours."

Opal traced the title: *A Young Magi's First Book of Castings*. She touched the flower she had grown. It was real.

Power surged through her. Every casting was now within reach. She felt the web of life beneath everything. If she could find the right words and emotions, she could do anything.

"I get it now. I'm not afraid of Biriad anymore. I'm not afraid of anything. With this power I can fix anything. Why haven't any of you done that?"

Hwue placed a hand on her arm. "Careful. Down that path lies death."

Wanting to prove him wrong, Opal closed her eyes and reached along the threads of life. She felt a pull to the north. She sensed a growing darkness.

Certain it was Biriad, she pulled herself toward the center of the fear. If she could remember enough of the banishment casting, perhaps she could deal with Biriad now and be done with him.

A presence far larger, darker, and more powerful than anything she had felt flooded into her. Her stomach heaved. She was paralyzed in its presence.

"Opal!" Hwue was shaking her. "Are you alright?"

Opal stared at him, pale.

"I don't think so. I don't think any of us is all right."

29

GATHERING THE BROKEN

The day before Opal made her second casting, Flint walked the walls of Varsik Castle, watching men and women hoist the gate up the cliff and into place. It was a pitiful beginning to the army he envisioned, but a beginning nonetheless.

In the weeks since their arrival, Flint had uncovered much about the castle. He'd been shocked to see the walls still stood, until Alberoth's journals revealed why. A preservation casting held the stones together. Flint worked the casting again to be sure. The wooden gate hadn't survived the dragons, but thankfully, it was the only major repair needed.

Other issues loomed. His army grew daily. First came the prisoners he'd freed, trudging up the boulder-strewn road. They obeyed, though some had resisted at first. Then more arrived, civilians fleeing Biriad's horrors. Flint had unleashed the primal wolves on nearby towns, driving survivors north toward the seeming safety of Varsik Castle.

Technically, the castle's location sat high in the mountains of the Northern Realms, outside Andrin's borders. Its proximity to dragons had always kept people away. No longer.

Flint magically seeded dreams across the region with visions of a savior in a mountain stronghold. The terrified masses came, staring at their dead ComScreens, dressed in city clothes too thin for the wild terrain. Accustomed to comfort and machines, they arrived ragged and weak, desperate for protection from the chaos behind them.

But they brought almost no food, and food was power. Magic demand-ed energy. Every casting drained him. The Living Throne of Power, Al-beroth's unlimited supply of energy, would've solved everything. Instead, Flint was stuck teleporting raiders to scavenge supplies, burning through energy faster than he could replenish the food. He could feel the edge of his power fray with every casting. Without the throne, his rise was slow... too slow. And somewhere in the mountains, Biriad waited, unpredictable, insatiable.

Still, things progressed. For now, refugees arrived slowly enough that he could meet with each one. He played the benevolent leader, listening to their stories, comforting them, pretending to care, while noting which ones could be bent to his will.

Pearl stood out. Young, well-liked, always smiling, always helpful, at least on the surface. But Flint saw beneath the gloss. She used cheerfulness as currency, always positioning herself, always reporting others' failures. There was grit beneath the shine. And that grit was useful.

He began drawing her in. He spoke of dark forces amassing to destroy Andrin, of the need to resist. He sent her to the library to study Alberoth's methods. She had yet to realize Flint was the dark force she should fear. Most people couldn't grasp that they were the villains. By the time Pearl understood, she'd be too entangled to leave.

She could also prove useful while he was gone. Leaving a power vacuum was dangerous, but Pearl would fill in nicely in his absence. She would be eager to help, but would never try to take his place.

He needed to go north. The dragons had noticed his growing activity; it was only a matter of time before they attacked. Flights drew nearer every day and there was a constant feeling of being watched.

Flint had read Alberoth's records of his dealings with the dragons. He felt sure he could win them over. When a scout appeared circling the mountains, Flint climbed the highest tower and reached out mentally. The reply dropped him to his knees.

Why are you in our land?

He fought back waves of fear, finally gaining control. The mental voice was not speech but raw understanding.

I seek a meeting to explain my presence.

He had been granted an audience with the dragon council.

Now, Flint strode along the wall, gazing north toward the peaks. Soon, he would climb them. First, he needed to find Pearl. He entered the library where she spent most of her time.

"Pearl?" he called.

She glanced down. "Yes?"

Her voice chirped with an unnatural cheer that irritated him.

"I'm heading out. You're in charge."

"Will you be gone long?"

"Hopefully not. Found the book yet?"

"There are dozens like you described. Leather-bound, with crests. That's not much to go on."

"Keep looking. How's housekeeping?"

"We've got another hundred single rooms ready. Twenty family rooms will be done by the end of the day."

"Good. Make sure to record all new arrivals while I'm gone."

"Don't worry. I've got it."

She rummaged through a stack of books and held one out with a smarmy smile.

"I thought this might help. It's Alberoth's casting prep for his first meeting with Dragon Lord FangClaw."

His smile was tight. Flint hated how easily she could mimic empathy. It was his trick, and now it wore someone else's face. He took the book and left.

"Good luck," she called cheerfully. "I'm sure you'll be fine."

Flint wasn't sure he would be fine. FangClaw was long dead; but his great-grandson, TalonStrike, ruled now. Flint could only hope the grudge over Alberoth's betrayal hadn't been passed down.

Back in his chambers, Flint packed nutrition bars and energy drinks. He skimmed the book Pearl had given him. He would study it more tonight.

He spoke a transportation casting while gripping a shard of stalagmite. In an instant, he reappeared inside a cave far to the northeast.

Out of curiosity, Flint attempted to nestle the shard into place in the base of the stalagmite it had been broken from ages before. It no longer fit; centuries of continued dripping had altered the shape of its source. He tucked the shard into his backpack, to return to the display case in Varsik Castle, ready to be used by the next person who wanted to visit this cave.

The air was damp. He conjured a yellowish orb of light with a whispered casting and followed it deeper inside. Near the back, a preserved side chamber waited, its magic defenses still intact. He cleared them and stepped inside: a stone slab bed, wool blankets, a ledge with an oil lamp, and a small leather-bound book with a raised crest.

His breath caught. His fingers trembled. The last transport casting had left a buzzing in his bones he couldn't shake. He needed food, or rest, or both.

But all he could think of was that he had finally found it and so he barely slept. He read through the night, planned his castings, stuffed himself with food, and readied himself for what might be the last thing he ever did.

At dawn, he hiked to the summit.

Dragons ringed the mountaintop like sentinels. They watched him climb. Their purpose was clear - make the supplicant feel small and tired. By the time he reached the top, his heart pounded, legs ached, and fear clawed at the edges of his mind.

And then he saw TalonStrike.

The Dragon Lord towered over the other dragons, all of which towered over Flint. TalonStrike was a mountain of obsidian scales and steel-blue underbelly. Viewed from below against the daytime sky, he'd be nearly invisible. A deadly hunter. His claws were the length of Flint's forearm. His gaze, ancient and pitiless.

Flint approached the center and called out.

"Great King of the Dragons, Lord TalonStrike, I request an audience of equals."

The dragon snorted, smoke curling from his nostrils.

"Equals? In what way are we equals? Can you fly? Can you wipe out an entire village with one breath? You live a blink of my life. You are not my equal."

"I cannot fly as you do, but I can fly. I cannot kill as easily, but I do kill. My life may be brief, but in it, I will do great things."

"Such as?"

"Conquer Maelandris. And perhaps Surubai, if I have your help."

TalonStrike roared, flames bursting from his throat. The air above Flint's head sizzled, but he stood his ground.

"You are a fool," the dragon snarled. "Why would we help the Drin?"

"Because we've surpassed you. Our airships fly faster than you. Our weapons can bring you down from miles away. And yet we have left you in peace."

He mentally projected images of sonic cannons, the new weapons arrayed at Varsik Castle.

TalonStrike lifted his head and roared another blast of fire, this one just above Flint's head. Flint willed himself not to duck despite the heat and the smell of burning hair.

The furnace stopped.

"A slight tilt of my head and you would be ash now. We are not equals."

"At close range, yes, but I can kill you from miles away."

The dragon stared. Flint didn't blink.

Finally, TalonStrike spoke.

"We will never help the Drin."

"Then don't. Just don't interfere. Let my army move south unopposed. When I rule, we'll sign a treaty ensuring your freedom forever."

Silence. The dragons turned to TalonStrike. Flint sensed them communicating. The pause dragged. He felt a sudden pull along the stream of life. It was strong and nauseating. Something wasn't right.

Opal? Had she learned so much already?

He pushed her back.

TalonStrike's gaze returned.

"We find this acceptable. We will ignore your presence. Should you come into power, we will renegotiate."

"Thank you, Lord Dragon."

Flint bowed, casting himself back to Varsik Castle.

Relieved at the truce with the dragons, he was still unsettled. This girl had become a genuine threat. He barely dropped his pack before rushing to his worktable. He had much to do.

War was coming sooner than expected. He would bring it to Opal first.

30

FIRST STAR

Opal's fear from the encounter with the powerful force had faded. She'd learned so much in the past few weeks, though she struggled to hold onto the words and feelings of castings. At times, the words felt slick, like they were coated in oil; ready to slip from her grasp at any moment. Even so, Hwue seemed pleased with her progress and kept saying their time together was almost done. Opal felt proud of her accomplishments.

Not all was perfect, though. She loved living with the Aellivi but missed her dad. Reconnecting with Will had helped; it made her feel like she had a family again. Still, she wished she could wake up in her bed and hear her dad singing in the kitchen.

Now she was savoring a moment of peace, sitting in comfortable silence with Hwue on a grassy hillside after a long afternoon wandering the woods. Cali's scree pierced the air. The drago circled overhead. He'd only been gone a few hours and must have found his supper quickly. The Aellivi had strict rules as to what he could hunt and had explained it to him. Opal couldn't wait until she could speak to him. For now, she could only pick up his general emotions. At the moment, he was sleepy.

She lifted her forearm. Cali circled downward, landed gracefully, hopped up to her shoulder, curled his tail around her neck, and tucked his forehead behind her ear.

Hwue lay back, chewing a blade of grass. Opal would miss him. They'd become good friends. She turned to him.

"Will I get to see Agent Bowman again before I leave?"

"Yes." Hwue said. "He's been learning much the same as you, though a bit slower, being an adult. He's studying with Master Magi Uerno in the High Hills and you'll be joining them."

"He got a master magi, and I got an apprentice?"

Hwue smirked. "An apprentice who was ahead of you when we started. Besides, how would you have reacted if some white-bearded elder told you to sit on a rock?"

"I probably would have taken it a lot more seriously."

"Exactly. And you'd have built your belief on his authority. Instead, you found truth for yourself. That foundation won't crack if I vanish tomorrow."

"I get that," Opal said. "Does Bowman have magic ability? I thought he was just a government paper-pusher."

"He has almost as much ability as you do. He wanted to go to Pascam, but his parents wouldn't allow it. Now he's finally learning to cast."

"If only I could have traded with him, we both would have been thrilled. But good for him. Maybe someday I'll finally get to learn physics."

"Maybe," Hwue said with a grin.

As the sky darkened, Opal scanned for the first star to make a wish on. A few months ago, the forest at night would have terrified her. Now it was her safe place. As long as she could tap into the life around her, she could take care of herself. In the city, she'd felt disconnected. Now nature was her whole world. She couldn't imagine wasting even an hour staring at a vidscreen.

Finally, a twinkle appeared above the trees. She hurried to speak before Hwue saw it.

"Brave first star in the sky, grant my wish before I die. And if it is within your might, bring my wish before first light."

"Shoot, I missed it," Hwue said. "What did you wish for?"

"I wanted to wish for my mom to be alive again," she said softly. "But I know that can't happen. So I wished for my dad to be safe until I see him again."

"That's a good wish, Opal. May it be granted."

Hwue glanced toward the mountains. "There are rumors that war is coming to Andrin. They've been preparing to strike at Flint's army north of the border. No one knows where. Just whispers on the stream."

Opal frowned. "But hasn't he taken in refugees? Would they really attack their own people?"

"Flint's power is growing. They can't ignore his attacks."

Opal hugged Cali a little tighter and lay back on the grass. Cali adjusted his position and snuggled close to her neck, already drifting back to sleep.

Stars spread across the dark sky. Opal's eyelids drooped. Cradled by the land, surrounded by a forest brimming with life, covered in a canopy of stars, she was content.

Then everything disappeared.

The sky. Cali. Hwue. Gone.

A crushing weight pressed her down, knocking the air from her lungs. She struggled to breathe. A cruel chuckle echoed through the blackness. A face emerged.

"Hello, Opal," said a man with a smirk. "My name is Flint. I'm truly grateful for your gift of Biriad, but now I have to kill you. I'm sorry." He laughed. "No, I'm not sorry."

Opal's mind grasped desperately for a casting. If she could just control her terror, she wouldn't need to speak. Just focus. Words bubbled up. She seized them and shoved against Flint's presence.

With a pop, she stood.

Air poured into her lungs. She shouted a casting, power rushing through her and exploding from her hands. Flint was flung backward in a wave of force.

Yes, this is why she had come to Aelliviss. This is why she had studied. Her destiny was to be a slayer of evil and defender of the kingdom. She launched into another casting to engulf Flint in fire.

But her words faltered. Flint locked eyes with her. Her body obeyed him. She stumbled forward, struggling to cast.

Pain ripped through her.

She collapsed.

"You don't learn, child," Flint said, looming over her. "You play with the power that feeds the universe. You think you know something? You know nothing. Go back to the source and try again."

Flint lifted his arms, beginning a casting she didn't recognize. But she understood enough; he was pulling her life into his own.

Her body burned. She wanted it to end. She thought of her dad. Of Will. She wished she'd been kinder to them, wished she could say goodbye. She wanted to warn them of the danger. She couldn't let them be hurt by this man.

A spark of defiance lit inside her.

She would not die at Flint's hands.

Through the agony, she scraped together the words of a shielding casting. Line by line, she muttered them, even though she felt no power. Flint was right. She was a fool to think she could fight the darkness.

Flint's chant faltered. His brow furrowed in confusion. He staggered back. Then the void yawned behind him and swallowed him whole with a pop of air.

Opal collapsed, gasping. Her skin prickled like hot cinders embedded under her flesh.

Shapes reformed: stars blinked back into being, and the smell of crushed grass filled her nose.

She blinked. No flames. No wounds.

"Opal!" Hwue's voice pierced the darkness. He sprinted toward her.

She croaked, "Here."

Then the world went black.

31

FLINT! FLINT! FLINT!

Flint caught himself on the edge of the table in his study, breath ragged. His casting to steal Opal's power had been broken, and he had no idea why. The floor shook beneath him. A deep rumble rolled through the walls.

Another explosion. This one nearer.

Varsik Castle was under attack.

Flint bolted to the battlements. Fighters streaked overhead, dropping bombs. Most exploded beyond the walls, but a few slammed into stone, sending up showers of debris. His ears rang with the shockwaves. Screams echoed through the castle. His army, what there was of it, was dying.

Why weren't the sonic cannons firing?

He sprinted along the ramparts to the first cannon. A nearby blast had killed the gunner. The others had abandoned their posts. In the courtyard below, there was chaos. Civilians screamed and scattered, clawing for safety.

He muttered a casting to amplify his voice.

"If five of you are brave, we can save the castle, and all our lives."

A few looked up, stunned. Most ignored him, scrambling for cover. Only one man moved with purpose. He was stopping others, trying to calm them. Flint recognized him. A dungeon survivor. Stone.

"Bring me four good people," Flint shouted to him.

Stone stopped a fleeing woman and spoke calmly to her, pointing at Flint. She hesitated, then climbed the stairs. Stone followed with three others. A bomb detonated farther along the wall, spraying dust and shrapnel. Everyone ducked. Flint's preservation casting had held. The walls groaned, but stood.

Once the air cleared, he barked orders.

"Aim here. Pull this to fire. Don't stop until every last fighter is out of the sky!"

They scrambled to the cannons. Soon, sonic blasts filled the air. Fighters began falling, pilots ejecting, gliding back toward Andrin. Within minutes, the surviving jets peeled away and fled.

A cheer rose. People emerged from hiding and gathered in the courtyard. Ash drifted down from the air. The smell of burning jet fuel singed his nose.

Pearl burst through a side door, flushed and breathless.

"We just received a message that ground troops are moving into Loevashn. They're setting up a base. We think that's where the air fighters went."

Flint's rage surged. He nearly let loose a fireball right there in the courtyard. Cowards. All of them. How could he lead a war with people who fled at the first sign of danger?

They had no discipline. No fear of him

That would change. Now.

He lifted his arms and shouted, amplifying his voice with fury. "I am ashamed."

The crowd stilled.

"Ashamed of myself," he said. "I invited you in. Promised you safety. And when danger came, I failed to protect you."

"But you did!" someone shouted.

"No," Flint replied, "Stone and these four heroes did. I failed to prevent the attack. I didn't believe Andrin capable of such cruelty as to attack its own citizens rather than aiding us in fighting the true evil."

He let the accusation hang.

"Today, we saw their depravity. I can only conclude that they are behind the karuk and his packs of primal wolves."

A tremor passed through the crowd. Grief twisted to rage.

"My gran died because of them!" someone yelled.

Flint seized the opportunity.

"We have word that Andrin troops are occupying Loevashn. From there, they're spreading across the kingdom."

More voices rose in anger.

"But I am also ashamed," Flint continued, "that I have not trained you better. I won't lie to you. You were cowards today."

A ripple of unease swept the crowd.

"That is my fault," he said quickly. "I didn't prepare you. That ends now. From now on, you will train. You will become soldiers. You will learn discipline. We will fight the evil that has become Andrin, and take back our kingdom."

The courtyard roared approval. Pearl was already beside Flint, pumping her fist with exaggerated zeal. But her eyes flicked over the crowd, gauging who was watching, who was slow to cheer, and who might be useful. She chanted his name with the others, but her smile never reached her eyes.

"Flint, Flint, Flint, FLINT!"

The name echoed through the walls.

Flint stood still, drinking in the sound like it was fuel. Power surged in him, not from magic, but from belief. These people were his now, and soon, the kingdom would be his, too.

32

THE DARK PATH

Opal emerged from the blackness to whispers. Cali nuzzled her cheek, grounding her. She opened her eyes. A ring of faces leaned over her, including Bowman, Will, and Hwue.

"Are you okay, Opal?" Hwue asked.

She wanted to answer, but her body felt distant, hollow. She focused on her voice.

"No," she croaked. "I can't beat him, Hwue. Not ever."

One of the older Aellivi leaned in. "Was it Flint?"

Opal nodded, remembering the searing pain and terror.

"I'm sure that's who I felt the other day. It wasn't Biriad after all. And this time he tried to kill me."

Several in the circle exchanged urgent whispers, then one of them ran off into the darkness.

Her head cleared enough to suddenly see Gale Bowman. "Agent Bowman?" she said. He smiled and squeezed her hand.

"How did Flint find me?" Opal asked.

"When you reached out to him, he learned where you were," Hwue said. "He and Biriad are working together. Biriad likely sent him to finish you."

"What stopped him?"

Hwue shook his head. "I don't know, but you can no longer stay in Aelliviss. Flint knows this land well. He can transport himself here without warning. You must leave now that he knows you're here. It's sooner than we hoped, but the time has come. You must go to Cavri."

"I'm not ready," Opal whispered. "I'm not sure I'll ever be ready."

A bearded, older Aellivi stepped forward. His presence was steady, commanding.

"There is no choice," he said. "As long as you remain here, you are in danger."

She hadn't been introduced, but the bearded Aellivi standing beside Bowman looked every bit the master magi she'd pictured. That had to be Uerno.

"If you can sense Flint, why don't you go after him?" Opal asked.

"That is not our way," Uerno replied. "We Aellivi do not attack. We only defend. Should Flint enter our forest again, we are ready."

"Then why can't I stay? You'll keep me safe."

"We cannot be certain we can. You must go now."

"One of you is coming with me, right?"

Uerno shook his head.

"Flint will not stop. He has tasted power, and he will not rest while others stand in his way. We can protect you best from here."

Queen Areu arrived with several Aellivi, each carrying packs. Hwue handed one to Opal. She stood and slipped it over her shoulder.

Queen Areu held out another pack to Will.

"Will," she said, "Liwan tells me your morning dream showed you with a choice to make. I ask you to make that choice now. I cannot see your path. You still have more to learn, but that learning might come with Opal, or it may come here. What do you choose?"

Will looked small and uncertain, shifting from foot to foot. His eyes welled up, and he blinked rapidly. Opal moved closer and took his hands.

"Please come with me, Will. I want you to come, but I'll understand if you choose to stay."

He didn't answer. His gaze darted to Liwan, then back to Opal. His lips parted as if to speak, then closed again. After a long pause, he gave the slightest nod.

"I'm going with Opal."

Opal exhaled. Relief and gratitude filled her. She turned to Bowman.

"Will you come, too?"

"I'm sorry," Bowman said. "I had planned to, but it's too soon. I need to stay here. I won't be much help to anyone until I finish my training."

He hugged her tightly.

"Thank you for bringing us here," she said.

"You're welcome," he replied. "I should say the same to you."

He pulled back and met her eyes.

"Be careful out there. Listen to Will's dreams. Don't do any castings until you're with the Cavrek. You'll be fine."

Opal turned to Hwue.

"Thank you for everything. You're a really good teacher and friend."

"And you are an excellent student and someone I am proud to call friend. You're welcome in Aelliviss always."

"I'm probably about to go through a growth spurt soon," she said, smirking. "I'll be back when you raise the ceilings."

They both laughed. Hwue touched his forehead to hers.

"Be safe, my friend. The next time we meet, the world may be very different."

Will slipped on his pack. They stood side by side.

"Flint may be watching. We can't send you magically and reveal your destination." Queen Areu pointed to an opening in the trees. "Follow that path to the river. A podder is waiting. It will take you downstream to Akro, in Cavri. Ask for Susev. He will take you to the city of Korova, where you will continue your training with the Cavrek known as Coras."

"Thank you, your Highness, for everything."

The tears streaming down Will's and Liwan's faces, told Opal they'd already said their goodbyes. She took his hand and gripped it tightly.

"We'll be okay," she said, hoping it was true.

At the tree line, they turned to see the friends they were leaving behind. Queen Areu, Bowman, Uerno, Liwan, and Hwue smiled with sadness. Each brought hands to forehead, then heart.

Opal and Will turned, and stepped into the forest. Opal thought she heard distant dark laughter echoing between the branches. She shook it off. Just the forest. Just nerves.

33

NOT YET

Biriad sat high on the mountain overlooking Varsik Castle. Fires flickered below, turning much of the recent repair work to ashes. The battle was finished. The fighters had flown home. One by one, the flames dimmed, then vanished. He would wait a little longer before returning to Flint's chambers. He was tired of the man's tantrums.

An explosion interrupted his thoughts. A fireball erupted from a small hut that had served as a temporary armory, lighting up the figures scrambling to douse the flames. Humans really were quite entertaining. Always dashing about, scheming, acting as if their lives mattered. He could snuff them out and the ball of dirt they crawled on would keep on spinning. Comical creatures.

Flint was the most amusing of all. At first, he'd seemed bent on revenge, hungry for power. But since reading Alberoth's writings, he'd started rambling about bloodlines, destiny, and some divine right to rule Andrin. Biriad had listened for a while, then stopped.

Flint still had value. As the kingdom fractured, Biriad would let the man draw his lines, name his enemies, and raise his army. Then Biriad would take it all.

A shadow passed overhead. Biriad looked up but saw nothing. Still, he was certain a dragon scout had just flown by. He didn't know how Flint had kept the dragons from attacking. They watched constantly, yet showed no concern about an army on their doorstep. A reminder that Flint had secrets. And leverage.

Biriad descended the mountainside, arriving at a fork in the path. The left path seemed to be a dead end. The right curved down toward the castle. He took the left, continuing to a slab of rock leaning against the cliff face. He slipped behind the slab and into a hidden entrance

He stooped as he moved through the tunnel. There was no light, but his karuk eyes picked out every detail; scorch marks on the ceiling from long-dead torches, nicks in the stone where weapons had scraped the walls. He knew every twist and passage. The tunnels let him meet Flint in secret, and spy on him in silence.

He passed by junctions leading to guest quarters and arrived at Flint's chambers. Voices carried through the wall. Through a slit, he saw Flint scolding his inner circle. The group looked like beaten dogs braced for another blow. Biriad scanned their faces, assessing potential allies. Some were off-limits. Goat, for instance. He had been one of the first to report to Flint. Seemingly loyal, Biriad suspected that loyalty would vanish once Flint did.

He was still considering Pearl. She played the naïve child well, but Biriad sensed that after her initial protests she'd align with power.

Then he spotted a new face. A man with bowed posture but sharp, calculating eyes. Flint called him Stone.

Ah, Biriad thought. *The dungeon holdout.* Strange to see him here. He must have said something clever, or dangerous, to rise so quickly. His body language said obedience. His eyes didn't.

Distrust was useful. And ambition was even better.

The meeting ended. Flint paced the room alone, muttering. Biriad triggered a hidden latch, and a panel slid open behind a tapestry. He stepped through to find Flint already facing him, arms crossed, furious.

"Where have you been?" Flint hissed.

"Delivering terrified citizens, as usual."

"Where are they?"

"Last I saw, they were being driven up the road. They should arrive by morning."

Flint resumed pacing. "Hopefully the Andrin troops didn't bomb them, too. Why would they do that? Their own people! Still... it does my work for me. I almost had her. But I can use this."

Biriad waited, silent. Eventually, Flint stopped pacing and faced him fully.

"I have a mission for you. It won't take long, and you can bring back more troops."

Biriad said nothing, waiting to decide if he'd obey.

"I had her," Flint said. "I was about to end her life when the bombing broke my concentration."

"Who?"

"Opal, you fool."

Biriad's eyes flared at the insult. Flint's face twitched as he caught himself, visibly tamping down his temper. Even he knew better than to provoke a karuk.

"I found her in Aelliviss," Flint said. "She's getting stronger. I could feel it. If we don't end her soon, it'll be too late."

In his head, Biriad heard her voice. Not words. Not thoughts. Just a whisper of connection, taut and humming. For weeks it had been slack, barely noticeable. Now, it vibrated with raw energy. Primal. Untamed.

His summoner wasn't hiding. She was waking up.

"You're still connected to her?"

"I am."

"Can you find her?"

"I can." Biriad's tongue flicked across his needle-sharp teeth. His eyes gleamed.

"Then bring her back to me alive."

Alive? Flint had done nothing but talk of killing her. Biriad now saw the truth, and it stank of betrayal. Flint wanted her power to enslave him.

The idea of tearing him apart right here was tempting.

Not yet.

He didn't have his army. Not yet.

"I'll leave tonight," Biriad said, bowing slightly.

"Be quick. Create more refugees along the way."

Biriad swept aside the curtain and vanished into the tunnels. Once he reached open air, he loosed a roar of rage. Submitting to a human was almost unbearable.

He loped down the mountain, entertaining himself with thoughts of how Flint would die.

34

LEFT WAS THE PLAN

O pal gripped Will's hand as they made their way through the dark forest in silence. Cali rode on her shoulder, his head swiveling as he scanned the shadows.

Opal listened intently for any sign Flint might be near. The only sound was the soft rustling of leaves under their feet, though her pounding heart made it hard to hear anything else. So did the storm inside her. Over and over she mentally screamed at herself.

How could I be so stupid? Who do I think I am? A girl who can take down the most evil thing our world has ever known?

Did I really believe I could win?·

And now she'd gotten herself exiled from the one place that could teach her the magic she needed to fight Biriad. The Cavrek didn't have magic. They had technology. But how was that supposed to help her banish a karuk?

The only small comfort was that their journey to Cavri brought her closer to Surubai. She fell back on her old fantasy of disappearing to the southern continent, working on one of the plantations. The people who once lived on Surubai had migrated north across the land bridge to Maelandris long ago, but the Cavri still ran farms in the dangerous jungles there. The pay was good, because the death rate was high. Maybe she could send money home before dying gruesomely.

The sound of bubbling water snapped her back to the forest around her.

"Water," Will whispered.

"I'm not sure we need to whisper," Opal whispered back.

"So why are you doing it too?" he whispered again.

"I don't know," Opal said aloud.

They both flinched. Her voice had broken a silence that felt like protection.

They stayed quiet as the path bent toward the water and revealed a small podder, its sides rolled down. It was smaller than the one they'd taken with Roa to Acoena, only a single row of seats down the center. They agreed Will would row and Opal would steer. Cali glided from her shoulder to the front of the podder and began grooming himself.

Opal opened a compartment by the rudder to stow her pack and found a safety harness inside. Lying on top was a river map. She and Will studied it by e-torch. Someone had marked their route in red and written, *Whenever you reach a fork, keep to the left.*

Simple enough.

Opal tucked the map away and buckled herself into the harness. She had no idea if the river had rapids, but she wasn't taking any chances. Podders were designed to right themselves and shed water, but if they flipped, staying with the vessel was the only chance they had.

Will took a seat near the front to balance the weight. Opal's canvas shoes skidded on pebbles as she pushed the podder into the water. Will began to row.

They drifted easily with the current. Neither had much to do except stay alert. In the dim moonlight, they scanned for low branches, exposed rocks, and more importantly, subtle eddies hinting at hidden dangers below. Their early adjustments were clumsy, but soon they learned to read the water and glide into the calmer channels.

Cali rode the front like a figurehead, flapping for balance when they hit rough patches.

The river widened and the current slowed. Trees leaned in, heavy branches trailing into the water. Stars shimmered above and below them, reflected on the river's black surface. The air was thick with humidity. Water lapped at the sides of the boat. It felt as if they'd stepped outside of time. Had it been an hour? Five minutes? Neither of them could say.

"Look... Up ahead," Will said.

A blinking light bobbed in the middle of the river.

"Is it a lantern?" she asked.

"I don't know, but we're heading right for it. Should we steer away?"

"I don't think we can."

Suddenly, the water grew rough. A jagged rock loomed ahead.

"Go right!" Opal shouted, throwing her weight against the rudder.

The podder bounced hard, swerving around the rock. The current flung them back toward the middle of the river. The bobbing light loomed closer.

Will squinted upward and saw a pair of eyes glittering under a snarl of dark hair.

He yelled. Opal looked just in time to see a figure drop from a branch and land in the center of the podder. Cali shrieked and vanished into the night sky.

Will spun, raising an oar over his head. Opal lunged forward.

"Stop! It's me, Hwue!"

The figure stood, lifting a lantern to his face. It was Opal's teacher. She managed to stop. Will didn't.

His oar sliced through the air. Hwue ducked just in time.

The force of the swing spun Will off balance, and he toppled over the side into the churning water.

"Will!" Opal shouted.

She couldn't see him. Then faintly his voice echoed ahead.

Hwue heard it too. He scrambled into the front seat and started rowing. Opal scanned the darkness. She kept hearing Will's voice, but the sound never seemed closer.

They rowed hard. But Will was being swept straight toward a cluster of boulders.

Opal's stomach twisted. "We need to get to him now!"

She jumped into the rear seat and together they rowed, straining to catch him. When they drew near, Hwue dropped the oars, lunged forward, and grabbed Will's outstretched arm. Opal helped haul him back into the podder.

Nobody was steering and the podder drifted right, heading straight for a fork. The current pulled harder. They slid into a narrow trough, bumping off rocks. Opal scrambled to the rudder, trying to force them left.

"Help me!" she yelled. "We need to keep to the left!"

But it was too late.

By the time Hwue and Will got back into their seats, the current had taken control. The podder was headed right, and the roar ahead was un-mistakable.

"Waterfall ahead!" Hwue shouted. "Harness up!"

They strapped in. Hwue quickly closed the podder and sealed the flaps, but Opal was still exposed in the back.

Her heart hammered. The roar grew deafening.

Then, the podder hung in the air.

The podder shot through the mist, plunged twenty feet, and crashed into the churning pool below. Opal was yanked under, her harness biting into her shoulders. She held her breath, lungs screaming.

The podder burst back to the surface, smacked flat, and skidded to a stop in calmer water. Opal lay sprawled in the back, gasping. Moonlight glinted off a wide beach ahead. She forced herself up and steered for shore.

The flaps opened. Will and Hwue were fine. The harnesses had held. The podder had done its job.

They coasted onto the sandy bank. Opal unbuckled and jumped out to push. Will and Hwue joined her, dragging the podder onto dry ground.

Will pulled out an e-torch and checked the damage. A few scrapes, a loose frame. Nothing major. The podder had survived.

Opal called for Cali. A high-pitched scree answered from above. He fluttered down, landed on the podder, then hopped to her shoulder.

"He looks good," Will said. "Now we can go on."

"There's just one problem," Opal said. "We took the wrong fork because somebody jumped into our podder and scared us half to death."

"I was trying to make sure you saw me," Hwue said.

"You definitely succeeded."

"I was going to yell," Hwue added, "but I didn't see you, because you didn't have any lights on. Then you were right beneath me."

"Lights?" Will asked.

"Most people hang a lantern on the prow at night. Helps you steer."

"Oh," Opal said, sheepishly. "Did Queen Areu send you?"

She dared to hope they'd changed their mind... that she and Will could stay in Aelliviss. "Nobody sent me. I figured they didn't really need me to defend Aelliviss. I'm more useful with you. If you get into trouble, you shouldn't use magic, but I can."

Opal smiled. "Thanks, Hwue."

She felt better already.

She retrieved the map from the podder's rear compartment and held it out. Will lit it with his e-torch. The three of them leaned in.

The river fork they'd taken curved west, straight toward the ocean.

Opal's heart sank. They'd barely begun the journey. And already, they were off course.

"Figures. I got us exiled, and now I got us lost."

A shiver crept through her.

"Let's build a fire and get warm," she said, teeth chattering. "Then we'll figure out what to do."

35

WHERE DREAMS LEAD

Opal, Will, and Hwue slept in a loose triangle around the remains of a dead fire, with Opal's arms wrapped around Cali, the drago's head resting on her forearm.

Once they'd lit a small blaze, their clothes dried quickly. Warm and exhausted, they decided to leave planning for daylight. Despite the hard ground, the steady lap of water against the podder lulled them to sleep.

Now dawn coaxed the three travelers awake. Hwue opened his eyes first and watched as Opal, then Will, began to stir. They stretched and greeted one another. Will got the fire going again while Hwue rummaged through their packs for breakfast. Warm oat mash and fresh peaches would help get them moving.

While they ate, Hwue studied the map, hoping to find a way to get them back on course. This branch of the river led to the ocean through a narrow, dangerous canyon. Walking back to the original fork would mean steep, difficult terrain. It made more sense to follow the river west and pick up a trail to Rottoera.

As they packed, Opal glanced at Will. "You woke like a normal person this morning. Don't you dream anymore?"

Will smiled. "I do, but Liwan taught me how to control them, so I don't wake up scared."

"Cool. What did you dream this morning?"

"I saw where we need to go."

"Where?" Opal asked, instantly alert.

Hwue looked up from the map, his full attention on Will.

"We need to cross the river and go north."

Hwue shook his head. "I think you might be confused. We are heading south to Cavri."

"No. I know what I saw. There was a woman living in a snow-covered forest. She's waiting for us. She's important. We need to go North."

"According to the map, our best path is to follow the river to the Pio-Rott junction. From there, a trail leads to Rottoera, a two-day walk. That's where we'll get a boat to take us to Akro."

Will didn't argue, but he was silent the rest of the morning, brooding.

They packed the podder and pushed back onto the water. Hwue, an experienced river runner, took the rudder and guided them through several more rapids. The river narrowed, wild and fast. Cali flew overhead, away from the spray. The podder bounced and skidded between canyon walls as Opal and Will shrieked with a mix of fear and exhilaration. Hwue remained calm and steady, expertly steering them through.

The river widened and curved around a bend. A sandbar stretched off to the left with several podders lined neatly along the shore. Hwue guided theirs in, and they pulled it up beside the others. After unloading their supplies, they hiked away from the river and toward the forest above the canyon. Cali rode on Opal's shoulder.

"What happens to our podder?" Opal asked.

"It's a junction. Someone will use it when they need to go downstream. We'll get another one at Rottoera."

"But Queen Areu gave us that podder," Will said. "Aren't we supposed to return it?"

"I'm sure there will be more arriving in Acoena today," Hwue replied.

Hwue and Opal entered one of the oldest Aelliven forests. Will hesitated a moment, staring north before joining them. The trees here were far apart and massive, with pale green trunks wrapped in thin, flaking bark. Their sparse branches hung high overhead, some as thick as an Andrin oak.

Hwue loved all the forests of Aellivis, but this one most of all. His family was here. Many of the trees were older than the Great Kingdom Wars. They had witnessed generations. Hwue felt their wisdom rising through the ground and into his feet.

It didn't surprise him when Will picked up on it too.

"Ever since I came to Aelliviss, I feel like the trees are..." He fumbled for a word. "Awake. Alive. I feel them."

"They are alive. And awake. Everything is," Hwue said.

"But why didn't I notice back home?"

"Because you weren't awake," Hwue said. "It's easier here. You're not just walking through a forest. In Aelliviss, you're walking among our ancestors."

Will blinked. "What do you mean?"

"When we die, we're buried in the soil, and a seedling is planted over us. Every tree is one of our ancestors. That's what gives this place its power."

Will and Opal walked in silence after that. It was a common reaction when Drin visitors learned they were walking through a graveyard. But for Hwue, that knowledge never brought sadness. He found comfort in it. Someday, he would rest here too, becoming part of this quiet strength.

Late in the afternoon, the trees lost their vibrancy. The trunks paled. They faded to white.

"This is what I saw," Will said. "A cold white forest."

Hwue nodded. "That makes sense."

"Why are they white?" Opal asked.

"They're healers," Hwue explained. "Scattered across Aelliviss are ancient groves. This one is the oldest in the southern forest. Through their root network, they absorb disease from other trees. They're nearing the end of their lives and sacrifice themselves for the good of the whole. Magi

Oka cares for them, keeping them alive as long as possible. When the last tree dies, the caretaker often passes with it."

"That's amazing." Opal said softly. "And sad. And beautiful."

"I should have stayed," Will said, kicking a stick in his path.

"What do you mean?"

"I'm not ready. I was sure about that dream, but I was wrong. Liwan would have helped me understand it. I'm not going to be able to help you when you need it."

"You've helped me more than anyone," Opal said. "One mistake doesn't change that."

"It doesn't feel like one mistake. It feels like... maybe I don't belong here."

Hwue tried to set his mind to rest. "You belong here, Will. Don't ever doubt that. You just need to know you won't always get it right. Neither will I."

They continued to walk. Here among the white trees, the forest was silent. There were no birds or insects, only pale light filtering through the canopy. The floor was carpeted with white leaves. Surrounded by silver stillness and towering trees, Hwue always felt as though he'd stepped out of time.

Ahead, a large, dark house appeared between the white trunks. The contrast was striking. As they approached, they saw Magi Oka waiting.

Half Aellevi, half Cavrek, the magi was only three feet tall and nearly as wide, with thick, white curls that fanned out around her head. Sturdy ankles and round toes peeked from beneath her green robe.

"Good afternoon, Magi Oka," Hwue called.

"Hello, Hwue," she replied. "I see you brought company."

Up close, she looked older. There were more wrinkles than he remembered, but her pale blue eyes still sparkled.

"I hear you've been expecting us," Hwue said.

"I have."

She reached out and hugged Will like he was an old friend. He hugged her back without hesitation. Then she turned to Opal.

"And you must be Opal Hart."

"I am," Opal said shyly.

Cali squawked. Magi Oka laughed.

"You are a beauty," she said, reaching out. Cali lowered his head so she could scratch beneath his chin.

"You've all had a long walk and a longer adventure. Come inside. I've prepared rooms and a hot supper."

The large two-story house was actually more inn than home. Downstairs was a dining room, a cozy sitting room, and a kitchen. Upstairs, eight small bedrooms, each furnished with a bed and sink. Heavy, dark furniture filled every room. Thick curtains covered the windows, as if Magi Oka were guarding her home from the surrounding whiteness.

Since no other guests were present, each of them got their own room. After settling Cali in, Opal followed the scent of food downstairs.

The kitchen, unlike the rest of the house, was full of light. Magi Oka had set a small table with four steaming plates. Hwue inhaled deeply the scents of mushroom and pine nut stew, freshly baked bread, and the delicate aroma of sautéed coraebus beans. Many of his favorites.

Magi Oka knew something of what was happening with Biriad. Over the meal, they filled in the rest. The conversation turned to Will's dreams. Hwue listened, quietly surprised at how grown-up Will sounded. Both he and Opal had matured, especially Opal. She had made mistakes, but she was growing past them. Hwue felt a surge of pride. And then, just as quickly, pushed it aside. The journey wasn't over. Her success was not assured.

"So, young woman," Magi Oka said. "I hear you had a run-in with a former pupil of mine."

"You taught Flint?" Opal asked.

"Unfortunately."

"I should never have attacked him before I was ready. I'm sorry."

"You shouldn't have," Magi Oka agreed. "But it was a good lesson, wasn't it? Hard lessons make the deepest grooves. That one will stay with you."

"It will."

"Then it was a mistake worth making. And you're already a better student than Flint ever was. He was impetuous, stubborn, and cruel."

Opal continued to ask about Flint, eager for anything that might help defeat him.

By the end of the meal, Will was nodding off. Hwue helped him upstairs, guiding him carefully up the narrow staircase. Opal stayed to help Magi Oka clean up.

When Hwue returned, he heard them deep in conversation. He didn't interrupt. Instead, he tiptoed into the sitting room, found a soft couch, and stretched out, listening to the clink of dishes and the quiet voices from the kitchen.

Opal told Magi Oka about her battle with Flint. The magi asked pointed questions, drawing out every detail. Then she fell silent.

Opal began to cry.

"I'm afraid, Magi Oka," she whispered.

"Of what exactly?"

"I feel something hunting me. What if Flint attacks again? What if Biriad finds me? I don't think I can stop them. I'm not strong enough."

"You aren't," Magi Oka said gently. "It's wise of you to recognize that. Flint can't find you unless you reveal your location by using magic. But if Biriad knows you're training, he may strike now, before you grow stronger. If you can feel him... he's likely coming."

"What do I do? Just die?"

"I wouldn't recommend that until you're at least my age."

Hwue thought he heard Opal laugh through her tears.

"Now wipe away your tears." Magi Oka said. "All hope is not lost. When your enemy is more powerful, you must use simple tricks."

"Like what?"

"Don't attack where they're strong. And when they attack, use their strength against them."

"How?"

"I can't tell you until it happens. But when you face the karuk, remember what I've said. It may save your life."

There was a pause. Then the clink of the last dish. "That's enough for tonight. Off to bed."

Opal stood and pushed her chair in. "We took the wrong fork," she said softly, mostly to herself. Then she looked up at Magi Oka and added, "But it got us here."

"To just the right place," she replied.

Hwue had started to drift off. *I should go to my room,* he thought.

But when the lights clicked off and Magi Oka's footsteps climbed the stairs, he stayed where he was.

Within moments, he was asleep, dreaming of dragons, karuks, and mushroom soup.

36

THE PACK

Biriad had been running for nearly two days and nights, stopping only to feed. His long limbs allowed him to cover vast distances quickly. He'd seen the terrain shift from rocky mountains to wooded hills. Soon he'd reach Kogan's Waste, a desert with no life at all. He needed to feed again before entering it.

Early morning light glistened on the white plain he had to cross to reach the Zygk Mountains, where he suspected Opal was also headed. If he was right, he could ambush her in one of the narrow canyons. High walls. No escape.

But first... food.

The tall grass thinned as he neared the cracked, dry land. He closed his eyes and reached for Opal's presence. The closer he got, the more clearly he could feel her.

At first, there was nothing. Then, finally she was there. Moving South.

He still had time.

He veered right, heading into the barren hills.

Now deep in Cavri territory, he searched for miners or farmers. Modern humans were easy prey. They rarely fought back. A thin line of smoke drifted into the sky up ahead. As he crested a hill, he saw the source: not smoke, but fine dust pouring from a vent above a mine carved into the hillside.

Metal clanked below. The breeze from the shaft was cool against the rising heat.

Biriad stepped into the mine, heading toward the sound of machinery. The tunnel ran straight for a while, then branched. At the first junction, tunnels veered left and right. The noise came from the right, sloping downward.

A faint blue mist drifted across each tunnel entrance. It had no apparent source.

Biriad waved a claw through it.

A screeching alarm exploded.

Blinding lights flooded the passageway. The sound drilled into his skull and his skin vibrated. He clamped his claws over his ears, then dropped one arm to feel his way forward, staggering back toward the exit.

As he neared daylight, his vision adjusted. The alarm still screamed, but no longer stunned him.

He heard voices. Footsteps behind.

He burst into the open, head pounding, and scrambled up the hillside. Crouching behind boulders, he watched rifle-bearing Cavrek men and women pour from the mine entrance and sweep the hillside.

He had forgotten, again, that the rules were different now.

No more arrows and spears. Now humans had weapons that could actually harm him. And strange defenses like that blue mist.

Despite their weaknesses, humans were a nuisance. A dangerous one. They gave up their search and returned to the mine.

He needed to feed. Soon.

To his left, he heard the clicking of stones being dislodged, followed by a snort.

Walking down a path nearby were five mountain horses. Small and stocky, with split hooves and padded soles, they were built for climbing. Their mottled tan coats made them nearly invisible in the desert.

He fed.

When he finished, he left the carcasses scattered and leaned back to rest. The sun was higher now, the heat rising fast. From below, he heard a grunt. Not human.

The blood had drawn scavengers.

Biriad slipped behind a boulder just as a bristleback crept into view. It sniffed the nearest corpse, then dabbed a red tongue into a wound. It opened its mouth to reveal rows of serrated teeth and clamped onto the leg, tearing through flesh in a single bite. The beast shook its head and swallowed.

More bristlebacks arrived.

They were long-limbed, with hunched shoulders that made their heads hang forward. Loose skin flaps around their jaws gave the illusion of a constant grin. Bristled manes ran from behind their ears to the middle of their backs. They had catlike paws and long, muscular tails ending in spiked balls they used like maces.

Biriad smiled.

He wasn't worried about Opal's magical ability, but it couldn't hurt to have backup. And though he couldn't kill his summoner, the bristlebacks could, if he chose to go that route.

He stepped out from hiding.

The first bristleback looked up. Its yellow eyes locked with his.

Biriad held its gaze. Reached inside.

It stiffened. Then relaxed. He repeated the process with the others, folding each of them into his will.

Biriad turned and walked into the wasteland.

The vicious bristlebacks followed behind him like pets.

37

INTO THE DARKNESS

The next morning Opal woke to white light streaming through her curtains. She peeked out at the frosty-looking world outside. She'd never seen anything like it, because Maead only had a ten-degree tilt, most of the planet experienced a mild, stable climate year-round. Only the far north and south saw ice and snow. The white trees made her feel chilled inside, though the air temperature was comfortable. She also couldn't shake a feeling of dread. It clung like a shadow over her mind.

After a hot breakfast, she joined Will and Hwue outside, packs in hand. Magi Oka emerged in a long leather apron, carrying a wooden bucket.

The stench hit them instantly.

Will gagged and pinched his nose. "Ugh, what is that?"

"Fertilizer for the grove," Magi Oka laughed. "Animal and human droppings, fermented to perfection. Let me hug you while I'm still clean, before this stuff sears off your nose hairs."

She embraced each of them. When she reached Opal, she leaned in close and whispered, "Don't forget, turn his strength against him."

Opal nodded solemnly and shouldered her pack. No one was sorry to see the little magi wander away, ladling stink at the base of every tree.

They walked in silence. Opal, with her head down, watched her feet push through fallen white leaves.

"Is everything okay?" Hwue asked gently.

She hesitated. "I guess. I just feel bad, and there's no reason for it."

"It's probably Biriad," Hwue said. "His energy is dark. I've felt it too, brushing the edges of the forest. Try to shift your thoughts. Focus on castings that could defeat him. And remember, we're still in Aelliviss. We're safe here."

"And how long before we're not?" Will asked.

"We'll reach Rottoera by mid-afternoon. After that, we take a boat through Bilgak Swamp, which will slow us down. We'll likely cross into Cavri tomorrow."

Opal shuddered. She'd felt protected in Aelliviss. Now it felt like she was standing on a cliff's edge, wings strapped to her back, no clue how to use them.

She pulled a casting book from her pack and flipped through the pages. She reread the words for binding and skimmed every other remotely useful casting. But the words wouldn't stick in her brain. Every time she imagined casting while staring down Biriad, the lines unraveled and slipped away.

She closed the book and grounded herself, as Hwue had taught her. She observed.

The trees were pale but regaining color. Birdsong floated through the air. Elms, oaks, and pines mingled with the towering ancients. The trail sloped downward. A small pink flower nodded near the path. Pine needles softened her steps. The air smelled green and sharp.

The world felt new again.

With that, her mind cleared. She spent the rest of the morning discussing castings with Hwue, and practicing the ones he recommended.

By midday, they left the forest behind, continuing toward a flat expanse of shimmering water and reeds. In the distance stood a small Aellivi town on its edge.

"That's Rottoera." Hwue said. "And that's Bilgak Swamp."

Hours later, they stood on the Rottoera dock. Drin, Aellivi, and Cavri bustled all around them. Unlike in Acoena, no one stared at Opal. Outside the deep forest, Rottoera had become a trading hub. She was just another Drin here. Still, she kept her head down, avoiding eye contact.

"Will," Hwue said, "get three days' worth of food. Opal, come with me to find a boat."

They navigated the crowded dock toward a wooden shelter. Inside a high-beamed building, hammers rang out as boats took shape. One Aellivi sat astride a hull, pounding slats into a watertight fit.

"Hello," Hwue called.

The man paused and looked up. "What can I do for you on this beautiful day?"

"We need a boat."

He leapt down and extended a hand. "I'm Boatbuilder Soel. And you are?"

"I'm Hwue. This is Opal. There are three of us, heading to Akro."

"Follow me."

Soel led them through a back lot of boats in many styles and sizes. He pointed to a wide, flat-bottomed boat with bench seats and a blunt nose.

"This is ideal for Bilgak swamp," he said. "And it'll handle the small rapids between here and Akro."

"How much is it?" Opal asked.

"It's twenty-four feet long," Soel replied.

"No, I mean, how much does it cost?"

Soel laughed. Opal frowned.

"You don't need money, young lady," he said. "If people don't take the boats I build, I'll have no room to build more. And I love building boats."

"But doesn't the wood cost something?"

"My wife is a lumber hunter. She finds trees ready to be harvested and brings the wood to me. She loves that work. I love this."

Opal looked at Hwue. "But what about food and rent?"

Hwue raised an eyebrow. "Have you paid for anything since arriving?"

She blinked. "Oh. We haven't."

Soel pointed to a beam above the door, carved with flowing script:**"When all have joy, there is no want."**

"People do what brings them joy," he said. "And in the end, everyone has what they need."

Opal tried to process that as Hwue and Soel gathered helpers to carry the boat to the water.

She walked to the edge of the dock. Yellow reeds stretched across the swamp, creating the illusion of floating islands. Hwue had said they'd travel through this marsh before entering a maze of watery forest, then on into Cavri's desert canyons.

She thought of her life in New Andrin, rarely venturing beyond a few city blocks. She'd seen more of Maelandris on this journey than she ever imagined.

With the boat in the water, Hwue and Opal headed off to the market to find Will. She had more questions about the lack of money in Aelliviss.

"What if someone loves to do nothing?" she asked.

"I've never met anyone like that," Hwue said. "What a boring life that would be. Even dreaming in the sun leads to stories and inventions. And those are welcome."

"What if someone loves logicomps? You don't allow them here."

"People who love logicomps have usually spent time in Andrin. And if that's where their joy is, then that's where they should be."

Opal didn't understand how this could work, but the Aellivi seemed to have mastered life without money.

They found Will, loaded the boat, and pushed off.

"How far are we going?" Will asked.

"We've got four hours of daylight," Hwue said. "Enough to reach the swamp forest. There's an overnight there."

Opal had been excited. Swamps always looked exotic in books... mysterious and alive with hidden dangers.

Reality smelled like rotting salad and felt like arm pain. Rowing through the still water was a lot harder than floating downstream. The reeds were full of herons and otters, not secrets. The air was thick with decay. Cali stayed high above the stench.

Hours passed. A green smudge appeared at the horizon. An island of trees with exposed roots spreading into the water. Moss draped from limbs. Cranes perched on limbs called mournfully. Ripples spread to their left, indicating something large swimming below.

Even Hwue's eyelids were drooping. Everything felt gauzy and slow, as if the swamp was casting sleep on them. Opal wondered if they were drifting through a dream, or into one.

At last, Hwue pointed, "There's our overnight."

A massive dead tree had been hollowed into a tower of stacked sleeping platforms and a cooking area at its base. They ate in silence, then climbed to their bunks.

Opal leaned over to say goodnight, but Will was already asleep.

She couldn't sleep.

Every time she drifted off, Biriad invaded her dreams and fear jolted her awake. She lay still, listening to Will whimper in his sleep. Hwue, at least, slept soundly.

As light crept into the shelter, she gave up and decided to make breakfast. On her way down, Will woke with a scream. She scrambled onto his platform, wrapping him in a hug.

"You were talking in your sleep... terrified," she said. "Did you dream something?"

"I... I can't remember. There was something. But right as I woke up, it was like a heavy black curtain dropped. I tried to pull it away, but whatever blocked me was too strong."

Opal swallowed hard. That curtain. She felt it too. That smothering darkness meant Flint. Or Biriad. Maybe both.

Hwue repeated his usual advice: don't think about them. Focus on what you can control.

They ate in silence.

By late morning, the reeds thinned and vanished. Cali fluttered down to perch on the boat's nose.

Ahead, hills of brown grass and scrub brush funneled the river into a faster current. It was a welcome relief from rowing.

Opal looked at her aching arms. When she clenched her fists, muscles rippled. She smiled. She'd never had muscles before.

Conversation returned.

"What's that?" Will pointed.

"The Gateway to Cavri," Hwue said.

Two towering stone statues flanked the river. A fierce Cavrek man and woman, held a shared platter above their heads. It overflowed with jewels, tilted toward the water, as if ready to spill its treasure.

Cali dove through the arch.

"What odd statues," Will said.

"Not really," Opal replied. "My dad told me about this. It's a warning and a promise. Cavri is harsh, even dangerous, but if you're brave enough, it rewards you."

"That's beautiful," Will said. "Let's hope it's true."

They passed under the arch.

"Now look behind you," Opal said.

On the Cavri side, the statues transformed into gentle Aellivi, smiling, offering a platter heaped with food.

"Aelliviss promises hospitality," she said. "And it always delivers."

A ripple of worry ran through her. The arch was beautiful, and she was glad she got to see it, but that also meant she was no longer safe in Aelliviss' borders.

They floated deeper into Cavri. Cali rode thermals above them then drifted off to hunt. The cliffs closed in. The water rushed faster.

Hwue's face tightened. "Row!" he called.

Opal and Will obeyed, plunging into the rapids.

Opal's stomach twisted. At the worst possible moment, the darkness returned, heavy and suffocating. Her vision narrowed. She leaned over the side of the boat and vomited.

The boat slammed into a rock and lurched. She flew into the river.

Cold blackness swallowed her. White bubbles swirled around her face. She kicked, clawed, but had no idea which way was up. The current tossed her.

Then - air.

She gasped.

Sank again.

A hand grabbed her. Will hauled her into the boat.

She lay, coughing up water.

Hwue guided the boat to a narrow beach. They dragged her ashore. Hwue clapped her back to clear her lungs. Will rubbed her hands.

She couldn't speak.

Finally, she mumbled, "I'm all right."

Hwue crouched beside her, face grim. "You scared us."

Will pointed to the boat. A section of the side had caved in.

Opal turned away and stared into the canyon. Terror thrummed through her body. A black tide.

Even Will and Hwue, standing right beside her, felt a thousand miles away.

He was unraveling her.

She knew it was Biriad. The closer she got to him, the more cut off she felt from life itself.

Connection.

The Casting of Connection sprang to her mind.

She spoke the words.

"Kadu basea Maead aurenis..."

The words hit like a lifeline.

Warmth surged through her fingers, up her spine, into her chest.

Biriad's shadow still loomed, but it could no longer smother her.

The world shimmered. Light returned.

She knelt, pressed her palms to the ground, trying to draw energy. Even here, in this barren place, she got a trickle.

It would have to be enough.

Cali was still out hunting. Good.

She looked back at Will and Hwue. She loved them. But they couldn't help her now. Better to leave them behind. Keep them safe.

Her fingers shook.

One part of her wanted to collapse into their arms, delay this one more hour. But she knew what that would cost.

Her emotions, once slippery, now surged at her call. She made the freezing casting without hesitation. Hwue and Will stopped mid-motion beside the boat.

She wanted to run to them. To hug them. To say goodbye.

Instead, she turned away.

White light had greeted her this morning. Now the canyon swallowed it whole.

She walked into the dark.

Toward the enemy she had summoned into the world.

And this time, she wasn't calling him. She was coming for him.

38

No Way Back

B iriad crouched on the rim of the canyon, feeling the girl's fear beneath him. He also felt the ripple of her magic. He would need to be careful.

A snarl erupted behind him. Two bristlebacks were nipping at each other. Biriad snarled back. They quieted, bloody snouts resting on forelegs, eyes locked on him, waiting for instructions.

He liked these creatures even better than the primal wolves. Along the way, he'd had a bit of fun with some Drin university students, hiking on break. Their blood now stained the bristlebacks' snouts. Originally, he'd meant to use the pack to corral Opal, then discard them. But he'd become fond of them. He would take them back to Varsik Castle. He wondered if they could adjust to the cold, or if they'd die. No matter if they did, he still had the wolves.

He'd spent several hours studying the canyon and planning. His four-legged allies could handle the cliffs with ease. He had already sent four down, two on each side, to cut off any escape by water. Now he waved a paw and grunted. The last two bristlebacks launched past him like arrows.

If his timing was right, she'd be surrounded within minutes.

As he traveled south, Biriad had weighed his options. He wanted her dead. He would be completely free then. Flint wanted her alive for now, but could he trust his motives? Which was the best way forward?

He heard growling below. The pack had cornered the girl and would kill her if he ordered it.

He would have to decide soon.

***

Opal walked along a dry, graveled streambed toward a fifty-foot cliff that looked like it became a waterfall during heavy rains. The sliver of sky above was a cloudless blue, so she was probably safe... from the weather, anyway.

She could feel Biriad, somewhere nearby.

A more powerful magi could extend the binding field. She wasn't sure she could even complete the casting, let alone extend it. She needed to get close. The thought made her shiver, even in the warm afternoon. Still, she looked for a way up the cliff, repeating the words of the casting in her mind.

A snarl cut through her thoughts.

She whirled.

Two of the scariest creatures she'd ever seen were stalking her. Bristle-backs. She recognized them from vidscreen pictures. One barked, its jaw unhinging to an impossible width. It could swallow her head whole. She turned and clawed for handholds in the rock.

Fear pushed her upward. She scrambled onto a ledge, heart pounding, only to find two more bristlebacks snarling down at her.

Below, the first two were joined by two more.

Six bristlebacks now.

She couldn't freeze them. There were too many. She remembered Magi Oka's advice: *Don't attack where they are strong. Turn their strength against them.*

Their strength was in their numbers, and those jaws.

She spotted a narrow ledge, just out of reach to her right.

There was a levitation casting in *A Young Magi's First Book of Castings.* It was simple enough, but the timing had to be exact.

As the bristlebacks leapt, from above and below, so did Opal. She lifted herself magically onto the narrow ledge and pressed against the rock wall.

The beasts landed where she had been and, in their frenzy, ripped into each other. Blood flew. Snarls echoed. Bodies tumbled downward. Only one bristleback remained, shaking, blood-soaked, then yelping as it bolted from the canyon.

A shadow rushed in overhead.

Biriad.

He landed, saw the carnage, and roared.

His lips curled back to reveal rows of jagged teeth. His eyes flickered red to black to red again, mesmerizing Opal.

She looked away, forcing herself not to be pulled in. She wasn't ready to face Biriad. She didn't have enough power left to bind him. She couldn't even remember the words. She needed to try anyway.

She forced herself to be still, and began.

"Aga . . . goa . . . siklai . . . tog . . . bogdra . . ."

Biriad hissed, as if stung.

But the next words... what were they?

"You don't know it, do you, little girl?" he laughed.

She clamped her eyes shut. They were in there, if she could just slow her heart.

"Aga goa . . . siklai tog . . ."

Biriad roared again, taunting Opal. "Come down, girl. You've got nowhere else to go."

Opal glanced at the wall. A slab jutted out. Maybe she could climb it. She reached for it. It crumbled. She staggered, windmilling her arms, then lunged and managed to cling to the rock.

Biriad chuckled.

"I'm not going to kill you," he said. "Flint wants to talk to you."

Flint had already told her what he wanted to do to her. Being killed by Flint was no better than dying by bristleback, so surrendering wasn't much of an option. She turned to face him. She needed a casting. Any casting. She couldn't levitate again. She didn't have enough energy to freeze him. Would a fireball even work?

Then she saw it: a massive boulder, near the cliff's edge. It was high. But it might work.

She calculated the angle. He was strong, but was he stronger than a mountain?

His weakness was arrogance. He didn't think she could hurt him.

She closed her eyes, found her courage, and whispered:

"Maead boluswa teo su afura."

The massive boulder fell silently until it struck the cliffside. Biriad looked up, snarled... and was flattened.

The canyon shuddered with the impact. Stones rained down. Then silence.

Had it really been that easy?

She stared, stunned. Why had everyone insisted she needed to bind him when a boulder did the job?

Maybe he wasn't dead. Maybe he escaped.

She climbed down and stood frozen, staring at the boulder.

The canyon was quiet, except for her own breath: sharp, shallow, unbelieving. Her heart pounded in her ears. She had done it.

She felt... stunned. Hollow.

Then, slowly, she stepped closer. Blood pooled under the stone. One hairy, wolf-like foot jutted from beneath it.

A bubble of laughter escaped her lips, strange and unexpected. She kicked the foot. It didn't move.

"You're really dead," she whispered.

Then she kicked it again, harder this time, and let out a full, giddy laugh. She'd won.

She raced back to the boat. A few words unfroze Will and Hwue, who continued inspecting the boat.

Her voice trembled. "It's okay. It's done."

Will's brow furrowed. "What do you mean?"

"I froze you," she said. "To keep you safe."

Will's mouth dropped open. "You... what?"

Hwue stepped closer, taking in her shaking hands. "What happened?"

Opal smiled. "I killed him. Come see."

They followed her into the canyon and stared at Biriad's foot.

"It's over," she said.

But Hwue wasn't celebrating.

"What's wrong?" she asked.

"That's not how this works," he said slowly.

"He's smooshed flat. Look. He's right there."

Cali screeched overhead, spiraled down, pecked at the foot, and tried to tear off a bite. The flesh was too tough.

"See," Opal said.

Hwue frowned.

"Can we go home now?" Will asked, eyes bright. "I want to make sure my dad is okay."

Opal hadn't thought of that. Home. Her dad.

For a moment, she wanted to dance with joy, but then her eyes narrowed.

"I'm not going home," she said. "If I do, I'll be stuck at Pascam. The great girl magi who defeated Biriad. I'm going to Korova. To study physics."

"What about your dad?" Will asked. "He must be really worried."

"He can visit."

Will frowned. "What do you think, Hwue?"

Hwue was still looking at Biriad. Then he turned.

"You need to finish your training. This isn't over. Flint and his army are still out there."

As Hwue spoke, Opal thought she saw movement, as if a shadow was oozing up the canyon wall. It moved like Biriad, but his lifeless paw was right in front of her. When she turned to look, there was nothing.

She muttered. "Now that Biriad's dead, Flint doesn't need me. He knows I can't beat him. Flint's not my problem."

"He kind of is," Will said. "He's only free because Biriad let him out of prison."

She winced.

"I don't want to think about it now," she said. "I'm going back to the boat."

She walked ahead, kicking sand. She knew magic was real. She'd felt its flow and its power, but right now she was so tired. She wanted comfort. She wanted her old life. Her old self. She wanted to learn about space and physics and the universe, to play video games and go rolling, to sit on the fire escape at home and look at the stars. She didn't want to be responsible anymore.

Up the shoreline, she spotted something cowering against the cliff.

It moved. Then snarled. A bristleback, wounded and trembling.

She squatted for a better look. It bared its teeth, a constant growl in its throat.

She met its eyes. It was terrified.

Without thinking, she reached out.

It snapped at her.

Will walked up behind her.

"It's hurt," she said.

"Yeah, I can see that."

"It'll die if we don't help it."

"Let it."

She glared at Will, and stomped back to the boat. She returned, unwrapping a package of dried meat. She placed it just out of reach. The bristleback's nose twitched. Slowly, it began to crawl toward the food.

"It's not evil," she said. "It was just being used by evil."

She returned to the boat and Will followed.

"Opal, you need to..."

She spun. "What? What do I need to do? Because I did what everyone asked. I lived on a rock. I learned magic. I almost drowned. I got rid of the karuk. What else do you want from me? I just want to be a kid who's good at science again."

Will looked at her gently. "But that's not who you are anymore. We can't go back; we can only go ahead."

Opal glowered at him, trying to think of an argument, but she knew Will was right. She imagined her old life. How could she enjoy sitting on the fire escape and seeing only a handful of stars now that she knew how many there really were? How could she be happy in class when she knew how much there was to learn in the world? Or live in the noise of the city, cut off from life?

Will placed a hand on her arm. "I'll go with you to Korova. We'll do this together. Study. Defeat Flint. Then go home. Okay?"

Opal collapsed into his arms sobbing.

It poured out. Everything she'd held in for months. Shame, fear, frustration, loss, even victory. It all washed over her. She didn't care how it looked. It felt good.

Eventually, she wiped her eyes.

"Thanks."

"You're welcome."

Hwue appeared. "Let's get the boat patched," he said. "I'll get you to Akro and hand you off to Susev. Then I need to return to Acoena and let them know what happened here."

They worked in quiet rhythm. Distance settled between them as they knew their time together was coming to an end.

Once they were moving downstream, the river widened, and their conversation became light.

Will sang an Aelliven song and Hwue joined on harmony.

Opal sat backward at the bow, eating, staring at the receding canyon. She looked across the rolling desert hills then at the rugged mountains they were leaving behind. She longed to go back to the green forests of Aelliviss, or even farther back, to the Andrin plains. She dipped her hand unconsciously in the water and pushed against the current.

The current shoved back.

Will was right. She couldn't fight the current and return to who she was. She felt the loss, then let it go.

The sun warmed her face. Will's voice skipped across the water. Cali flew ahead, scouting what lay beyond. She had no idea what he saw... what was coming.

Right now, that didn't matter.

Right now was enough.

Pronunciation Guide

Acoena – ah-<u>so</u>-na
  Aellevi – <u>ay</u>-lih-vi
  Aelliven – ay-lih-<u>vin</u>
  Aelliviss – ay-lih-<u>viss</u>
  Akro – <u>ack</u>-row
  Alberoth – <u>al</u>-burr-oth
  Andrin – <u>and</u>-rin
  Areu – ah-<u>roo</u>
  Avo – <u>ah</u>-vo
  Belken – <u>bell</u>-ken
  Bilgak – <u>bill</u>-gack
  Biriad – <u>beer</u>-ee-ad
  Cavrek – <u>cav</u>-rick
  Cavri – <u>cav</u>-ree
  Deullen – <u>doo</u>-lin
  Hwue – hue
  Karuk – <u>care</u>-uck
  Korova – core-<u>oh</u>-va
  Liwan – lee-<u>wahn</u>
  Louir – lou-<u>ear</u>
  Maead – may-ed
  Maelandris – may-<u>land</u>-ris
  Mukdri – <u>muck</u>-dree

Oka – <u>oh</u>-kah

Pascam – <u>pass</u>-kum

Pio-Rott – <u>Pee</u>-oh-rot

Repticin – <u>rep</u>-ta-sin

Roa – <u>row</u>-ah

Roeterra – row-<u>ter</u>-ra

Surubai – soo-roo-<u>bi</u>

Varsik – <u>var</u>-sick

Vulkera – vul-<u>care</u>-ah

ACKNOWLEDGEMENTS

The seed for this story was asking what a high-fantasy world would look like after 2000 years of progress and technological advancement. Not long after, Opal's story unfolded. I am grateful for that spark that lit the fire.

I want to thank all the early readers. I won't name names, because this was written 10 years before publication. I don't remember everyone who read it then and I don't want to leave anyone out. But you remember my terrible, repetitive writing. Thank you for your patience and encouragement.

Thanks to my first editor, Patrick Merla. Your experience was so far beyond what I deserved and I am grateful you tolerated my ineptitude. I learned much.

I would also like to thank editor Juliana Brandt, who took on the project after my many revisions and helped clean up the mess I created.

Thank you to my cover artist, Marina Price. You caught my enthusiasm for this project and helped bring my vision to life.

I want to thank Jeff Walklin for being the first person to tell me how lucky I was to know my purpose, which was to write. I couldn't quite wrap my head around it then, but I so wish it to be true.

Thanks to Diane Hyronimus, my 'sister' who has been with me through so much of this life's journey. You always knew I should be writing books instead of screenplays. You are the strongest person I have ever known. I wish life had been more kind.

And thanks to my sister, Sherryl Ferguson, for always being a voice in my corner and a champion of my dreams.

Thank you to Jennifer Simpson, whose friendship has spanned decades despite you being way too cool for me. You have twice altered the direction of my life and I will always be grateful for the course correction.

So many thanks to my mentor and friend, Melissa Miller Young, who believed in me and helped change my career. You are an amazing champion of women, and have enriched so many lives, including mine.

And thank you to Susan Gilmore for never trying to reshape me. Because of you, I breathe easier in my skin.

Thanks to each and every person I have encountered in life, kind or cruel. You all shaped who I am, how I perceive the world, and the stories that leak out of me. You have all given me fodder for fiction.

If this adventure swept you away, leave a review to help other brave readers find the magic too.

If you want to know more about Maead and its people, please visit fearunleashedbook.com. Join the discussion on the message board and sign up for the newsletter to learn more about the two upcoming books that will finish the trilogy: Fear Rising and Fearless.

ABOUT THE AUTHOR

Lynnie DN is a writer and editor with a background in television production and a passion for storytelling. After supporting other authors through editorial work, she turned her focus to crafting her own fiction. *Fear Unleashed* is her debut novel. She lives in the Ozarks, where she continues to write, edit, and develop new projects.

www.ingramcontent.com/pod-product-compliance
Lightning Source LLC
Chambersburg PA
CBHW020631110726
47899CB00002B/733

MARVIN FOX

COLLECTED ESSAYS ON PHILOSOPHY AND ON JUDAISM

VOLUME TWO

Some Philosophers

Edited by
Jacob Neusner

Studies in Judaism

University Press of America,® Inc.
Lanham · New York · Oxford

Copyright © 2003 by
University Press of America,® Inc.
4501 Forbes Boulevard
Suite 200
Lanham, Maryland 20706

PO Box 317
Oxford
OX2 9RU, UK

Library of Congress Cataloging-in-Publication Data

Fox, Marvin.
Collected essays on philosophy and on Judaism /
edited by Jacob Neusner.
p. cm. – (Studies in Judaism)
Contents: v. 1. Greek philosophy, Maimonides —
v. 2. Some philosophers — v. 3. Ethics, reflections.
1. Maimonides, Moses, 1135-1204. 2. Philosophy, Jewish. 3. Jewish
philosophers. 4. Ethics, Jewish. 5. Judaism. I. Title. II. Series.

B755 .F67 2003
181'.06—dc21   2003048437 CIP

ISBN 978-0-7618-2530-2

♾™The paper used in this publication meets the minimum
requirements of American National Standard for Information
Sciences—Permanence of Paper for Printed Library Materials,
ANSI Z39.48—1984